INTRIGUING SHORT STORIES©

By

RIETTE SUZZETTE ORMOND
And
GEORGE ORMOND

All of the names and characters portrayed in this novel are fictitious, the product of the authors imagination, and any resemblance to actual persons living or dead is purely coincidental. However, the sites, places, and cities are factual and most are historical.

Riette Suzzette Ormond and George Ormond, Intriguing Short Stories

Published by Suzzette Exclusives, San Diego County, California

ISBN: 0-9620518-7-X

Front and Back Cover: Designed and Photographed by Riette Suzzette Ormond

Manufactured in the United States of America

MORE EXCITING WONDEROUS BOOKS
By
Riette Suzzette Ormond, B.A.
George Ormond, B.S., M.S.

FOREVER MY LOVE©

Cliff Camden, a handsome and wealthy lawyer, faces life without his wife, Julia, after she is killed by a drunk driver and leaves their two young children motherless. His secretary, Jane Simms, sees the tragedy as an opportunity to convince her boss that she should be his wife and mother to his children. Meanwhile, his New York law partners think Cliff should start a new life in California and open up their new west coast office in San Diego. Although Cliff has no intention of falling in love again, he meets a statuesque blonde named Claudette, Could this be his second chance for love?"

FOREVER MY LOVE is the romantic love story of three generations, how they interact, enjoy being together, sharing, and solving a variety of problems.

This romantic novel includes two adorable children Ra Ra, 4 years old and 18-month old Jacques. Ra Ra, short for Gabriella, loves to sit in her rocker singing to her dolly as she rocks back and forth. Jacques loves playing with his favorite toy Cuddles, the goose.

Unique Program
For
Staying Healthy,
Young, and Trim©

THIS IS THE BOOK
For
ALL Those
Serious
Health Conscious Individuals
who want to learn how to eat healthy.

It encompasses in detail
how the authors
in one day changed
their way of eating
to be healthier
by making
Healthy Food Choices.

Cuddles Helps Santa Claus Save Christmas©

Colorful Illustrations by Riette Suzzette Ormond

This is a Fun Loving Story that will keep you in Suspense!

**Complete with colorful illustrations
Featuring:
Elves in their workshop,
Mrs. Claus baking cookies,
Santa Claus relaxing in his rocker alongside
his grandfather clock,
Santa Claus and Cuddles,
A Medieval Castle,
All the toys,
and much more.**

**An Enjoyable Book for Children
of All Ages 2 to 102
that includes
Blank White and Red Pages for Children to draw, thereby
making their memories.**

A GREAT GIFT!

HO! HO! HO!

THESE

INTRIGUING SHORT STORIES

ARE DEDICATED

TO

ALL THOSE HAPPY PEOPLE

WHO ARE WILLING TO READ THEM,
ESPECIALLY THOSE WHO ARE

WILLING TO SPEND A FEW SHECKLES
TO BUY THESE STORIES.

AUTHOR'S NOTE

The fictitious characters are people who experience unusual events due to circumstances beyond their control.

IF IT WERE YOU,
how would you react if:
without warning you suddenly regress to a ten-year-old child who is returned to your former hometown where you know everybody but no one recognizes you?

OR, find yourself transformed into a Union general in the middle of the Civil War facing Confederate soldiers?

OR, facing a jealous army captain who confuses you with his supposedly immoral wife whom he believes is servicing male army personnel, and is ready to kill you with his pearl-handled army revolver?

AS YOU READ ON,
YOU WILL FIND ALL THE ANSWERS...

INTRIGUING SHORT STORIES

By

Riette Suzzette Ormond

and

George Ormond

TABLE OF CONTENTS

THE BIRTHDAY GIFT©

A ROMANTIC MYSTERY
SHORT STORY

The Characters

Become involved in a series

of startling and

unexpected mysterious situations

which neither

they nor the reader

could have anticipated.

THE BIRTHDAY GIFT(c)

CHAPTER I

It was a day of excitement--a day of celebration and happiness--a day Melissa would never forget. she smiled knowingly and apprehensively as she felt a surge of uncertain pleasure.

Here it was after five long years--her 21st birthday. Don had promised a surprise. She asked herself, "Will it be the matching wedding ring set or the diamond bracelet?" She always admired the beautiful jewel pieces displayed in Le Seur's Jewelry Store window.

She purposely passed the jewelry store to admire the diamond studded bracelet elegantly displayed on a black velvet stand.

"I know I won't be disappointed. He has good taste," she rationalized trying to reassure herself while nervously pacing in the living room around and around the elegantly brocaded gold upholstered sofa, then lingering at the window, one hand absentmindedly stroking the heavy antique satin draperies while anxiously waiting for Don to arrive at the magic hour of seven. She was very much in love with the tall handsome ex-marine.

Earlier that week, the young couple made plans to celebrate her birthday: attend a musical play at the Latin Quarter, a quaint little theater, then enjoy a romantic candlelight dinner, and later dancing to a three-piece combo at the El Portal.

Six thirty, only a short time; the pretty blonde thought to herself, glancing at the star-shaped uniquely designed timepiece braced against the wall above the red antique brick fireplace, her excitement growing with every tick of the clock.

A cheerful glowing fire burned in the hearth, sending colorful sparks of yellow and orange light, simulating dancing fingers casting patches of light and dark shadows, creating illusions of chairs, tables, and sundry pieces of furniture, moving in non-rhythmic patterns.

The girl always enjoyed watching the soft glow of the comforting warm fire. Temporarily hypnotized by the burning logs and the cheery crackle of the flame, she paused for a second then turned her attention toward the large oval wall mirror and nervously began arranging her hair while closely examining her face and touching up her make-up.

After studying her image more closely, she continued pacing. Several minutes later she forced herself to sit down, but relaxing was not in her schedule--time slowly stretching out so that seconds seemed like hours.

"Six forty five. Only fifteen minutes--not much more time to wait." She thought looking at her dime-sized diamond wrist watch then glancing at the front door.

The television program temporarily distracted her. Melissa had become oblivious to the droning of the weatherman's warning of an impending rain storm. The newscaster's voice was one of those deep, resonant voices that you only expect emanating from a television or radio broadcast.

"Ladies and gentlemen, we interrupt this program to warn you that a heavy storm is heading our way. It will hit Westville in approximately one hour. Flooding conditions may exist. Please drive carefully...And from the nearby Westville Air Force base a Captain Jack White is on trial for the murder of his wife..." "Such violent people, and I abhor violence," she thought to herself as she sat on the couch. Her preoccupation erased the weatherman's prediction.

His monotone irritated her. She promptly left the couch and turned off the electronic apparatus, returned, relaxed against the mountain of pillows, closed her eyes, and fell asleep.

The crackling of the burning logs broke the silence of the semi-lit room, awakening her several minutes later. Melissa's blue eyes wandered to the antique table and the open book that she had started reading earlier.

"The Old Mansion on the Hill," why had she chosen to read such a depressing novel, she couldn't remember, and at this time cared less.

A sudden series of knocks at the front door distracted and startled Melissa.   A shiver ran down her back. Her heart beat increased in intensity. She sprang like a new-born colt running impatiently to open the front door.

Pausing to regain her composure, Melissa stood for a few moments at the front door; a feeling of apprehension overcame her, uncertain of the surprise that lay in store.

CHAPTER II

While smoothing her dress, she wondered: "Will Don notice her pink velvet strapless evening gown with the plunging neck line and be pleased with her new hair style?"

"After all," she rationalized, "This is the latest Hollywood style. I want him to be proud of me.   And, I bet he'll love the fragrance of the perfume I'm wearing even though it has a stronger scent then the kind I used on our first date," she assured herself, feeling confident that Don would be pleased.

She opened the large engraved brown oak door, trying not to overreact, acting cool and composed, and sublimating her nervous and impatient feelings.

Melissa's sky blue eyes sparkled, seeing Don standing in the doorway pleasantly surprised. The scent of her perfume filled the air, intoxicating him with delight. She stood a tall girl, a few inches shorter than Don, honey blond hair softly flowing around her shoulders and down her elegant back.

The six-foot handsome former marine captain was speechless for a few moments as he was standing there in his white tuxedo jacket and black bow tie. He smiled down at her thick shinning blonde hair spread across her bare shoulders, the way her long blonde lashes enhanced her blue eyes, the red softness of her lips, at her attractive cleavage where smooth flesh and gown met, admiring her beautiful cherubic face, and silhouetted curvaceous body hypnotized him.

He was finally able to speak and said, "Melissa you look beautiful," a faint smile parting his lips and a look of excitement in his eyes.

Melissa's eyes sparkled, a light pink blush colored her lightly rouged cheeks. "Come in, darling, come in," she exclaimed. The bright moonlight illuminated Melissa's smooth white skin and accented her trim figure.

Don extended his arm, grasping Melissa's hand, eagerly entwining their fingers, gently slipping his other arm around her small waist and walking side-by-side into the living room.

After they settled on the couch, he placed his arm behind her; then monopolizing her attention, framed her pretty face with his hands. "Close your eyes. You have such beautiful eyelashes, and I like to look at them," Don softly whispered as he lowered his mouth down to her, pressing his lips against her tender moist red lips lovingly kissing them long and deep. His kiss took her breath away, a strong sensation flooding throughout her body.

He lifted her chin and moved his fingers along her chin, a feather-light touch. His eyes gleaming with friendly humor, he handed her a golden plastic box. "This corsage will compliment your new evening gown and hair style." He leveled a penetrating look at her, and then played with her earrings, barely touching her skin.

Melissa's eager hand snapped up the florist box, opened it with her other hand and removed its fragrant contents. "Gardenias! My favorite flowers," she shrieked with delight, lifting the flowers and holding them close to her slightly up-tilted nose. "They smell heavenly. Thank you, Don, Thank you," She repeated, her bright eyes smiling.

With a gentle caress, he drew her closer to him, placed her cheek against his broad chest and held her, overwhelming her with desire to hold on forever and almost going on past morality.

Unwelcome thoughts passed her mind. However she could not fight her strong principles of chastity and reasoned that after their marriage, she and Don would enjoy the matrimonial and emotional ecstasy they would experience in their own private bedroom.

"Virginity is precious. Don't waste it on a frivolous affair," mother advised Melissa during one of their mother-daughter talks. She made a vow to remain chaste and practice abstinence as long as she was single. She did not allow her hormones to overcome her common sense.

"Darling, in that sexy evening dress and with that hair style, you'll be the talk of the town, and your perfume will really knock the guys out."

Melissa raised her head and looked up at Don's well-defined classical strong features. In front of his brow a small auburn curl loosely hung. She reached up and tweaked the lock of hair.

"Melissa," he smiled at the gentle teasing touch and protested as he playfully grabbed her hand.

"All right, you grouch." Melissa loved teasing Don. They sat silently for a moment facing each other.

She felt Don's arms embracing her, their lips passionately kissing, and then reluctantly separating. "Here is Don," she thought to herself, "a successful lawyer, holding, caressing, and kissing me." They sat hand-in-hand.

"Melissa, you have the prettiest hands I have ever seen or felt."

"Thank you, Don. You say the nicest things; Darling, I love you very much."

She examined the corsage, trying to find the pin. "Where is the corsage pin? I can't seem to find it. I guess the florist forgot to put one in the box. I'll find one. There should be one somewhere in this room."

She scouted the room for a straight pin. Nearby on an occasional table a lead crystal dish contained a variety of small and large pins. "Here's one," she announced, reaching out and picking up the metal sliver.

"Here, Mel, let me pin on the flowers."

He carefully pinned the flowers to the waist of her pink velvet strapless formal, "You make the flowers look beautiful," Don exclaimed, admiringly. "You're like a beautiful work of art. Darling, I'm so lucky," he said.

CHAPTER III

The couple sat on the couch, embracing and kissing. Their gentle kiss went on and on, for a minute, for an hour, it seemed; then silently they held each other for a few minutes.

Once again Melissa became exuberant. The turning point in her life had arrived. She dreamed of this day when she would be in the arms of the man she loved since her senior year when as a cheerleader she watched her football heroes win games while cheering them on to victory.

This was the moment depicted in movies when the handsome actor marries the beautiful movie heroine.

"Sweetheart, close your eyes," Don suggested.

Melissa closed her eyes, playing his game.

Don quickly reached into the inside pocket of his jacket, withdrawing two black velvet covered jewelry boxes, one slightly larger than the other.

Anxiety overcame composure. "Oh, Don!" Melissa feeling very nervous waited impatiently to see what precious tokens Don had in store.

"Keep your eyes closed and cup your hand, palm up. No fair peeking," he insisted softly, holding the velvet containers behind his back. "All right, Mel. Open your beautiful eyes."

Melissa opened her eyes and laughed quietly at Don's little charade.

"Which hand?" he asked. The young woman hesitated for a moment.

"Let...me...see. I, think I'll choose the right one," and touched Don's arm.

He pulled his arms forward, placing his hands near his chest, fists clenched, fingers wrapped around the smaller box while depositing the larger box on a nearby coffee table.

Melissa's curiosity overcame her patience and reached for the object.

"Not yet, Melissa. Touch the invisible button on my left elbow and see what the magic will do for you."

At the light touch of the elbow, Don deftly moved his hand forward, placing the jewel box in Melissa's cupped hand.

She grasped the box carefully and excitedly opened it, revealing its contents--a heart-shaped gold locket and chain.

Removing the jewel, she admired the small ruby encircled by six minuscule diamonds embedded in the center of the gold heart; deftly she pried open the locket.   Individual photographs of the couple were encased in each wing.

"It's beautiful, Don. You are not only wonderful but thoughtful," she murmured, turning her attention toward Don. A look of pleased satisfaction spread across his face.

"Ya ain't seen nothing yet," he mused. "Look on the back."

The girl closed the locket and eagerly turned it around.

"Please read the etched inscription aloud. I love the sound of your sweet voice." Melissa obliged: "My Darling Melissa--let the light of our love brighten our future lives forever, Don."

"How beautifully poetic." Her eyes welled up and a lone tear slid down her soft roughed cheek. Gently cupping his hand around the girl's dimpled chin, Don raised her face to his, removed the falling tear, and with a gentle touch, pressed his lips on her forehead in a loving fashion, as a loving mother kissing her adoring child.

At the feel of his hand holding her face, she began a free fall of delight, desire, and something close to her. A warm sensuous feeling raced through her slim body. Her breathing increased. Her knees weakened. For a moment she felt like wax, melting, allowing her emotions to run away as a love-starved child awaits her mother to embrace her.

"Here let me put it on," Don interrupted her emotional rapture, bringing Melissa back to reality. Taking the locket from Melissa, he slowly placed the thin gold chain around her petite neck and snapped the clasp to secure the locket. He placed his hand affectionately on her shoulder, admiring the jewel. Triumphantly, he announced, "Hmm, just what the doctor ordered."

The gold metallic object nestled in her cleavage, emphasizing the closeness of the girl's half-covered bosom. Her smooth white skin complemented the glistening jewel. She fondled the small heart rapturously, feeling the diamonds, ruby, and etched inscription, toying with it like a child with a new toy as pearls of tears flowed in small dribbles from her eyes; a swift smile overcame Don's serious projection.

"A perfect fit," Don said, drawing Melissa against his broad chest gently drying her teared eyes.

"Oh, Don. How did you know? I have always dreamed of owning a heart locket. Thank you."

He complimented glibly. Melissa smiled joyously. Nothing she had experienced felt as delicious as her first meeting with Don at the school dance.

CHAPTER IV

Don reached toward the nearby coffee table for the other jewel box, picked it up and handed it to the girl. "Here Melissa. The best is yet to come."

A faint smile pervaded over his serious expression. She eagerly grasped the velvet box, then slowly and carefully pulled open the top.

Breathlessly she examined the contents. "Oh, darling," she exclaimed ecstatically. "A set of matching rings!" she screamed with delight unable to suppress her elation.

"Surprised!" he said excitedly, kissing her cheeks and lips. He paused for a moment and in a firm voice whispered in her ear, "Darling, I love you, will you marry me?" He waited for the words to sink in.

Melissa failed to understand the question. The fascination of the rings locked her concentration.

Don waited through her silence for an answer. He touched her arm, bringing her out of her concentration. "Will you marry me?" He repeated more forceful, redirecting her attention to him.

For a single surprising moment Melissa looked at Don. The message--loud and clear--became embedded in her mind.

This was the ultimate wish come true when your loved one proposes to you. "Oh, darling, of course I will," breathlessly she exclaimed with delight. "I will!" She repeated, "I will!" Her heart pounding with joy.

The couple faced each other for a few moments in a warm embrace, kissing passionately, Melissa repeating softly, "I love you. I love you, darling. I love you very much. I do! I do! I do!" then turned their attention to the contents of the jewelry box.

"Here sweetheart, give me your hand," Don said as he removed the exquisite engagement ring from the satin lined jewel case. Melissa thrust her left hand forward, ring finger fully extended outward.

Holding the girl's hand, Don held the ring between his thumb and fore finger, slid it on her finger past her evenly manicured red fingernail.

He half-smiled. "It matches your personality. A perfect ring for a perfect girl." he complimented, caressing her hand intently."

"It is a perfect fit." Melissa was awed by the ring's snug fit. "But how did you know my size?"

"You remember during our last date when I held your hand?" "Yes, I remember. What about it?" "Well, I curled my index finger around your ring finger without any suspicion on your part."

"Pretty sneaky, Don. I should have guessed."

***"Now you know the secret," he said. At arm's length the half-carat diamond reflected thousands of pin point light rays overshadowing four small diamonds encircling the primary stone on the setting of the engagement ring.

***The newly engaged girl moved her hand several times in a half-circular motion, admiring the ring's reflection and the enhancing effect of her newly enriched well-tapered finger.

"I must admit, Mel, the ring looks much better on your finger than in the box."

"Now, let's try on the wedding ring." He removed the ring from the opened box and anxiously slid the band onto her finger.

"Oh, Don," Melissa sighed deeply, admiring the two rings. "They are beautiful!"

Don pulled Melissa toward him and kissed her hand. "Anything for you, malady, ask and it shall be yours."

CHAPTER V

Momentarily Don's hand disappeared into his tuxedo's wallet pocket, reappearing with a pink envelope clenched between his fingers. "I had almost forgotten," he apologized. "Here," he said, "Happy birthday, Mel."

The pink envelope aroused her curiosity. The many cards and letters she had received in the past were encased in white envelopes, but never in color. She opened the envelope and pulled out a diamond-shaped card, four distinct pages hinged together.

A large diamond and a poem were imprinted on the face of the first page. "Please read it to me, Mel. You are very good at reciting poetry."

"Certainly Don, here goes." Melissa cleared her throat and read ceremoniously,

> My Darling Melissa,
> We promise to each other to be true
> To spend the future just with you
> To share together day and night
> And make our happiness a new delight.

The next page displayed the outline of a red heart and two gold metallic paper rings intertwined and affixed in its center. Handwritten poems filled the spaces of the interior of each ring.

"Page two, Don," Melissa advised, her eyes clouded with happy tears. Pausing momentarily, she wiped the small liquid globules then continued reading each poem individually.

Sweetheart,
This love I give to you
A married life that's new
To live forever in your heart
Always near you, not far apart
and
Love, honor and respect
My dearest I expect
To share each sweet caress
With tears of joy and happiness
And fill each day and year
With fond memories so very dear.

Melissa cleared her throat and read ceremoniously:

The third page depicted a vertically expanding three dimensional panorama: a paper house situated on the page accented by green grass, a small bed of colorful flowers surrounding the home, and four small figurines--a man, a woman, a boy and a girl--each peering out of red trimmed windows.

Melissa pulled open the simulated red tile brick roof and saw the four miniature paper figures surrounded by replicas of miniature furniture.

She opened the paper door cautiously with her index finger and peered inside at the minuscule inhabitants and contents. A feeling of enchantment and fascination overcame her as she alternately and repeatedly opened and closed the tiny door and roof.

For a few minutes the house seemed to come to life and made her feel like a child playing with the doll house she once owned before a fire gutted her former residence and its contents. "I was a child when I lost everything I treasured, everything" she recalled.

Momentarily depressed, she finally closed the small door, turning her attention to the printed verse at the bottom of the page.

Don noticed the change in the girl's face as an imperceptible sigh escaped her, "What's the matter, Melissa?" Don asked, becoming quite concerned. "Did I do something wrong?"

"No, Don, you didn't. Just living in the past....I guess. I am all right now," Melissa whispered, her tinged red eyes shedding tears, regained a stoical control of her emotions; a smile replaced the indifferent far away gaze. Her calmness was an act.

The lack of inflection in her voice bothered Don. She reconciled the past with the present and fought off the melancholy that had temporarily clouded her feelings.

"Poor baby," Don said sympathetically, his extended arms gently fitting her warm face into the hollow of his shoulder.

She finally relaxed not wanting to end this moment of endearment. "I am fine," Melissa insisted, feeling warm and comfortable.

"Are you sure you are all right now?"

It was a gentle question softly whispered as sympathetic as a mother asking a child with a slight fever.

"Yes, of course." She nodded her assent. Her words were indefinite, smiling dubiously.

Don did not fully accept her reassurance but played her little charade.

The girl became more enchanted as she read the verse:

Remember Dear
Our plans will be
A girl, a boy or two or three
Our house will be a home
With a happy family.

then slowly turned the page.

A map entitled "Our Honeymoon Travels" was printed on the back of the last page. Small arrows, strategically located, illustrated geographical locations of leisure, enjoyment, sports, and rest areas all within the confines of theaters, parks, hotels, and restaurants. Silently she studied the map with its narrow and broad thoroughfares. There was something excitingly familiar. Suddenly her memory supplied the missing pieces of the puzzle. "It's Harbor Cove!" she screamed, raising her hand, putting it over her lips in an attempt to stifle her enthusiasm.

She fondly recalled the delicious time she had as a child when her family traveled to the small metropolis. The security she felt as she slept on her mother's lap during the long drive to Harbor Cove where the family members enjoyed boating and canoeing from shore-to-shore on the small lake as she watched the floating lilies, arched wooden bridge, and thick blanket of green grass covering the nearby picnic grounds.

The group satisfied their hunger in a small restaurant where in the adjoining patio Melissa sat, eating tasty foot-long hot dogs, in a child-sized replica of an eighteenth century locomotive engine while admiring the hues of multicolored flowers and shrubs surrounding the richly decorated courtyard filled with happy diners occupying quaint tables and chairs.

A periodic visit to the existing museums became an exciting adventure.

The wax museum--Melissa's favorite--depicted horror and ghostly scenes of historical, legendary and literary events, where her elderly grandmother detailed each of the character's--the Marquis De Sade, Genghis Khan, Nero, Brutus, The Borgias, the Headless Horseman and others--motivations and movements, filling voids with fantasies and characterizations, making the individual settings come to life, creating an aura of mystery. And for many nights, sleep became difficult. Nightmares filled with the wax habitants engulfed Melissa's dreams.

Reflections of the past were suddenly interrupted, leaving the little girl behind.

"Well, Honey, what do you think?" he inquired, pointing to the map.

Melissa smiled a little, allowing a moment of silence to pass. "This is all so beautiful," and pressed her lips against his, kissing him affectionately.

Her eyes returned to the booklet, quickly scanned the map and read the printed verse at the bottom of the page:

This map is our romantic story
Of love and life in all its glory
Engagement, marriage, and a honeymoon
As husband and wife so very soon
And soon thereafter there you'll see
The children of our family.

Melissa slowly closed the small birthday booklet, drew it toward her chest and held it.

Silently, Don took her hand and kissed her slender fingers. He smiled and took from her the birthday booklet. Her heart beat so wildly, she could hardly breathe.

Don cupped her chin and turned her face to his, and the lovers exchanged glances. Then staring at her sparkling face for a moment and stroking her honey blond hair, he rested his pleasant eyes on hers saying, "I hope this small gift expresses my true feelings for you."

Smiling, she finally said, "I can't think of anything more wonderful than the lovely gifts you have given me. This day will live in my memory forever. I will always cherish this time for the rest of my life." She gave him her sweetest smile, tightly winding her arms around his neck and lifting her soft mouth to his and kissing him.

"Shall we set our wedding date?" Melissa asked

CHAPTER VI

Don shot a look at his golden wrist watch. The time had passed quickly. "Look, darling," he said anxiously. "It's almost eight. Fix your face and let's get going. We can discuss our wedding plans tomorrow."

"By the way, Mel, I know we planned to go to the Latin Quarter and the El Portal, but at the office one of my clients said there is a new nightclub at the lake. The seafood is superb and it features the "Neptune's", a five-piece combo well-known for its musical arrangements. The group has played in all the top night spots in the country."

"What's the name of the night club?" she asked, her eyes flashing with excitement.

"The name of the night club," continued Don "is the Coral Reef. It is built on a small island in the middle of Colonial Lake. The exterior is very picturesque. The interior walls are lined with fish tanks. Soft lights beam through the tanks while music plays, creating the illusion that fish and sea life are swimming and dancing to the rhythm of the music.

"The dance floor is a huge glass plate covering an immense aquarium with two compartments: One containing baby sharks; the other, a large variety of fish. A marbled sea shell forms the band stand at the rear of the dance floor. Soft lights flash from beneath the glass surface keeping rhythm to the music as couples dance romantically while the fish swim lazily.

"It feels pretty weird as though one is dancing in the middle of the ocean. A recording of the surf plays in the lobby and the rest rooms, giving the atmosphere a touch of realism.

"Finally the dance of the Hawaiian maidens dressed in authentic garb completes the floor show."

"Sounds dreamy and romantic," she added, "and candle light too, I suppose?"

"Oh, yes. Just the way we like it," answered Don, his voice deep and resoundingly warm.

"Darling, let's go to the Coral Reef and celebrate," Melissa agreed. The change of plans pleased her.

She reluctantly removed the wedding ring from her finger and inserted it in the velvet box; then grasping the jewel containers and birthday card, crossed the living room.

She stopped at a provincial three-drawer desk. From the top drawer, she withdrew a red leather box containing cards from previous birthdays and assorted mementos and distributed the latest additions among its contents. She reflected for a few seconds slowly, closing the leather case and returning it to the drawer.

"Ready, Melissa?" A note of impatience enveloped Don's deep voice.

"Yes, Don, I'm on my way!"

"I forgot to tell you," he explained as the two lovers walked side-by-side toward the door, fingers entwined, "The band plays personal requests. I'll ask them to play two pieces--one for your birthday; the other for our engagement. And get this....the kitchen serves cakes and treats for special occasions."

The fire from the fireplace quenched, lamp lights darkened, front door locked, and the celebrants left the house.

The stars were coming out of their hiding place, while the full moon played hide and seek above a few purple clouds.

CHAPTER VII

"Welcome to my chariot," joked Don inviting his fiancée to enter his car while opening the door on the passenger side.

"Don, this is a beautiful automobile. When did you buy it?"

"I purchased it few days ago. I wanted to surprise you. Please get in."

Melissa entered the car and sat in the bucket seat.

Carefully pulling down the safety belt, Don buckled in his fiancée.. "Comfortable?" He smiled, placing his arm around her shoulders and kissing her.

"Yes, Don, thank you," Melissa affirmed. He then entered the driver's side, sat down, closed the door, buckled his safety belt and asked Melissa, "All set?"

"Yes Don. Let's go. I know we'll have a great time," Melissa said, happily peering out the windshield of the very expensive silvery convertible.

The full moon outlined the countryside hills as the car sped west along the two- lane uneven asphalt ribbon leading to the main highway through a valley where orchards and farms dotted the landscape and sheep fed greedily in green pastures. An orange grove still bright with oranges and several ponds speckled with ducks and geese came into view illuminated by the moonlight.

Don glanced at his fiancée resting her head uncomfortably against the cold window glass. "Just like sleeping beauty." He pulled the sleeping girl toward him, resting her head on his shoulder.

"Hm..m..m," Melissa mumbled incoherently. She looked at Don with half-opened eyes and sank back into sleep. The humming of the engine mesmerized Melissa into an illusionary dream world.

Mermaids--wedding rings on their fingers, gold bracelets entwining their wrists, and little bells dangling from their tails--swam in undulating movements past Melissa and Don standing on a wide platform, facing a huge diamond ring centered by two intertwining flaming hearts.

Their favorite song, "Our Love has Touched Us" was softly playing in the background, reminding her of the first time that she heard the tune at a school dance where she met Don who was visiting his younger sister.

"Excuse me," Melissa apologized, accidentally spilling a cup of grape punch while racing across the gym floor "That's perfectly all right, Miss," he said, drying his hand with his handkerchief.

His deep voice was flavored with a New England accent. Melissa admired this handsome Marine lieutenant. He was tall with broad square shoulders, distinguishing auburn hair trimmed neatly, a soft wave gently flowing through the center.

He noticed her shapely figure and shoulder-length honey blonde hair, as he continued on his way, becoming one of the dance floor crowd at the high school prom where Melissa was voted home coming queen, top cheer leader of the cheering squad, and Westville High's graduating class valedictorian.

The automobile sped smoothly devouring the small paved artery.

A sudden change of tempo and engine sound aroused the sleeping girl as the convertible slowed down, stopped at a "stop" sign, negotiated a short rise, and made a right turn onto the main highway.

"Where...are...we?" she stammered sleepily, trying to stifle a yawn; her eyes partially open.

"We've just reached the main highway, sleepy head. Have a nice nap?" he queried, as one talking to a child.

"Uh, huh, but it was too short," she complained, a tone of disappointment underlying her voice. "I could have slept longer. I hated to wake up."

A boyish grin appeared on her fiancé's face; he faced Melissa for a few seconds then forced his attention to the road.

In the distance the sky was laced with long streaks of rain clouds partially covering the moonlight, forming ghostly forms manipulated by some unforeseen heavenly spirits.

Long angry icy bright forks of lightning suddenly cut across the sky with satanic force accompanied by exploding claps of thunder.

Trees and grass played "hide-and-seek" as the couple motored along the broad highway toward the city. A gently meandering stream paralleled the highway. From her side window, Melissa observed flashes of lightning separating the tiny rivulet into separate disjointed fragments.

"Look, Melissa," Don said, distracting her. "We are coming to town." His index finger pointed toward the many tiny lights twinkling like flickering candles in some deep dark forbidden abyss.

The moon had now completely disappeared behind the numerous black clouds as the couple reached the first signs of civilization on the outskirts of the small metropolis.

The flickering changed into bright lights, a few at first then their intensity and numbers grew rapidly as the silver-gray convertible periodically stopped for red lights and then continued on its way through the city, past streets, alleys, avenues, broad boulevards, small and large shops, department stores, shopping centers, and fire stations. Red, yellow, and green traffic lights intermingled with street, neon, and store window lights displaying their abundant and colorful merchandise.

The two some were oblivious to the mingling local citizens walking, sightseeing, and shopping, flitting from store-to-store many carrying packages and parcels in rhythm to their own pace, time, and need.

The kaleidoscope of people, slow and fast traffic, thoroughfares and lights passed as Don and Melissa reached the outer limits linking the city route with the main highway directing the pair toward their designated pleasurable destination.

"How much further, Don?" Melissa felt uneasy as she peered through the windshield. The scattered rain clouds spread a gray and black curtain and droplets of rain began to fall steadily, creating tiny water lines on the windows. There was nothing outside to raise her spirits.

Don became aware of the uneasy feeling projected by his fiancée. "Won't be long now. We're almost there," he said, attempting to ease her uncertainty. "Don't worry about the rain. You know how quickly it rains then stops at this time of the year. It will clear up in a few minutes," he assured her, fervently continuing with the explanation.

"We'll be there very soon. The county recently cut and paved a small two lane road just a mile or two from here; and as you know the Coral Reef is built in the center of Colonial Lake. There is a large parking lot near the shore.

"After parking the car, a special motor boat ferries you to a tunnel leading to the nightclub entrance twenty feet below the surface of the lake. Then a glass sphere elevator transports you to the restaurant and dance floor.

"And get this Melissa! On the way up, fish swim all around the outer perimeter of the elevator. It's fantastic....truly fantastic. Anyone who goes there really enjoys the ride, food, atmosphere, floor show, and dancing.

"I know we'll have a great time," he concluded and drew a deep breath, hoping to ease Melissa's tension.

She felt relieved, totally at ease, and gave him a smile.

"You always know how to have a good time, darling," Melissa said, snuggling closer to Don. There was no question in her mind that the evening would indeed be perfect. His plans always turn out so wonderful. And, after all, this was a special day--her birthday and proposal of marriage. "What could be more wonderful? How could anything go wrong?" She thought to herself. "Besides he is such an excellent driver; so what's a little rain?"

CHAPTER VIII

The headlights of the vehicle cut through the darkness. Suddenly a small two-lane road appeared at the right, joining to the highway.

Slowly the car came to a stop. A small wooden sign inscribed with "Welcome to the Coral Reef. This way please turn to the right and go down the two lane narrow road."

"Make a right turn," she announced triumphantly, pointing to the right.

"Right it is, Oh! Great guide and master; it shall be done immediately, if not sooner," he joked, a small grin appearing on his face as he proceeded to enter the small two-lane semi-paved, graveled track.

The jolting of the car by the craters and rocks covering the surface of the partially completed route did not discomfort the occupants.

Thin sheets of rain increased slowly diminishing visibility. Small water puddles quickly began forming on the roadway, causing the wheels to periodically slide as the vehicle rolled ahead.

"Look, Don, we're coming to a forked road, better slow down." she advised quietly, somewhat dismayed.

"That's strange," Don emphasized quizzically. "No one said anything about a fork in the road." Don's concern and uncertainty became obvious.

Turning off the motor, he faced Melissa, enfolding her in his arms then taking her hand in his own.

A wall of rain hit hard against the automobile, creating an invisible translucent curtain on the windshield, minimizing visibility and blurring the countryside.

"Melissa," he continued, "Lower your window and see if you can find a road sign."

"Okay Don, turn on your bright lights, I'll stick my head out, and look around."

She opened her side window part way and stationed her chin on the rim of the glass, scouting the junction of the two roads for a sign or directions. Heavy drops of cool rain washed her face as her eyes explored the area where the twin roads met.

"I don't see any sign. Maybe the rain washed it away; nevertheless I can't seem to locate one."

"Neither can I," Don concurred; and concerned about her he suggested, "pull your head in and close your window. All you are doing is getting a free shower compliments of mother nature."

"What now?" she asked, following his direction while patting her face with paper tissues. The couple sat quietly for a few minutes, trying to decide what to do. The rain increased in intensity and began to beat down very loudly as lightning crackled and thunder slapped, casting an illusionary short lived Fourth of July. Darkness became more intense as the rain came down with yet more determined violence.

The trees and bushes swayed frantically with the erratic undulating movements of the wind and rain, making the night symbolically clear of the situation. Breaking the silence between the partners and Melissa looking to Don for guidance, she haltingly asked, "What do we do now?"

'"Flip a coin," Don answered precociously. "Heads to the left. Tails to the right."

"Stop kidding, Don. This is no time to be funny," scolded Melissa.

"No, I am serious."

Melissa raised her thinly curved eyebrows in surprise, looking at her fiancé. A shiver made her shake visibly.

"Are you cold?" Don asked fatherly.

A protectiveness she liked and had experienced several times before.

"Here, let me put my jacket around you." Removing his jacket, Don draped it around Melissa, his strong arm encircling her shoulders, drawing her to him. "There. Is that better?"

"Yes, Don, much better," Melissa answered, the warmth of his body made her as comfortable as a child in a crib.

"Why don't we go to the left?" Melissa suggested.

Choosing the left fork, they continued driving.

"Hope you made the right choice, Mel. Anyway let's see what the future holds."

The pounding rain and reverberating bass of thunder made the two lanes more and more hazardous as the torrential rain blanketed the roadway. Streaks of lightning cut across the sky, briefly illuminating the darkened terrain.

CHAPTER IX

The couple continued on, watching for some signs of civilization. The rain continued its loud drumming as they rounded several curves and finally came onto a straight stretch of road. In the distance Melissa caught a glimpse of small flickering lights shimmering through the darkness.

"Look, Don. Lights ahead. See them?"

"Where?"

"Look--in between the trees. Keep looking. You'll see them."

His eyes swept the distance. "I see them! You are right, Mel. I only hope they will let us in."

The movement of the trees allowed the small lights to surface between the shadows. From a distance flashes of lightning made a toy-sized building become more apparent.

A three-story plantation, partially hidden by decaying trees, finally came into full view when the vehicle reached its targeted destination and stopped.

The couple sat silently looking at the antiquated edifice, then faced each other. Breaking the silence, Don spoke almost apologetically. "Not the Coral Reef, but at least, I hope, we can stay tonight."

Long forks of lightning cast aside the inky darkness to reveal the decades of neglect suffered by this early seventeenth century brick colonial structure. Moon, sun, summer, winter, rain, and snow had eaten into the wood, warped the boards and peeled off the paint.

The darkness lit only by flashes of lightning as the storm moved on, the rumble of thunder gradually became fainter.

"Early colonial," she thought to herself, recognizing the architecture as being the same as her aunt's gracious mansion where she spent many happy days in the well-preserved, refurbished home.

Wide cracks deeply cut into the marble fluted Doric columns, once handsome, were now like some deformed tree trunks with perceptible fissures running chaotically and zigzagging downward from the tile roof and disappearing at the base. The walls were scored by enormous cracks; the water spouts broken. The once beautiful cast iron work was now rusted, bent, and several sections were missing.

The center of the marble steps was now deeply concave; the edges, crumbling and disjointed; several large pieces were missing. Many of the weathered bricks were now chipped. Some shutters were missing; the remaining ones were broken, unpainted, or worn.

Several stained glass window panes were taped; others badly cracked. The balconies were hung with birds' nests.

The same ruin prevailed throughout the dated and aging house, hopelessly in disrepair.

CHAPTER X

Melissa's mind momentarily wandered back to the time when as a young child her grandmother related a particular incident that occurred in an old colonial mansion several miles outside the city limits, involving a young army officer and his wife.

Time had concealed past memories of grandmother's tragic story about the young newlyweds. What exactly had happened was unclear, and this was not the time to relive the past.

It was late; the weather unfriendly; warmth and shelter a necessity interrupted her thoughts. "Don, looks like somebody is home. I just saw a woman's face looking out of an upstairs window. Maybe she will let us stay for the night. Anyway...it's worth a try."

He quickly opened the car door and ran, climbing the two short steps into the mosaic-floored portico. He lit a match and searched for a door bell, but none was to be found.

A large bronze metal knocker adorned the upper part of the richly carved splintered wooden door. Hitting the door with the metal ring several times, he paused. There was no response.

Impatiently, He directed a tremendous battery of violent knocks against the door and shouted, cupping his hands to his lips, "Hello... can you please...help...us." Still no response.

Melissa waited no longer. She quickly left the vehicle and ran to join him, announcing loudly, "I'm coming!" The couple stood next to each other. "Let me call," she urged. "Maybe she is afraid of men and won't open the door."

"Hello there!" Melissa shouted above the sound of the heavy downpour. "We need help! We are lost! We'll pay you to let us stay tonight!" She begged. "Please help us!"

The high ceiling of the small shelter afforded them safety from the elements. Minutes seemed like hours as the couple waited like trapped animals for a helpful answer to their desperation.

Suddenly the door opened slowly part way by a thin ring less hand; a flood of glaring lights temporarily blinded the newly engaged couple.

A low pitched, harsh, female voice projected through the partially opened door. "What do you want? What are you doing way out here? You should be home instead of wandering about on a night like this!" She scolded a cutting edge in her tone.

Melissa's heart beat heavily as she gripped Don's arm. "Please, please help us!" she repeated anxiously. "We lost our way and need a place to stay until tomorrow morning. The rain is making it impossible for us to find our way back. Please let us stay. We'll pay you if it is necessary!" She pleaded.

"Well...all right...come in!" Her deep voice, unfriendly and foreign, invited the lost unwanted visitors into the house.

The door opened very slowly revealing an elderly woman in her seventies. Melissa glanced nervously at their elderly hostess. Her lined wrinkled face was colorless as wax and narrow as two folded hands; it was evident that time had played over her freely.

Something besides years had had a hand in her aging. She was slim and stiffly dressed in a toe-length black dress that matched the darkness of the night; her head and back covered with a worn blue shawl as old as the woman herself, patches and streaks of gray hair appearing in complete disarray. Her thin black slippers lacked luster.

The couple entered the house cautiously and waited for the elderly resident to lead the way.

Melissa felt uncertain about the house-something sinister and disturbing. She felt as though she was back in the wax museum. Her dislike for the mansion grew every second.

For a moment, running away seemed a solution. However, would Don accept this sudden feeling?

"He would only laugh and make me feel childish for suggesting something was wrong," she admonished herself.

"Perhaps he would say, `You have been hearing too many stories from your grandmother; or `You're letting your imagination run away from reality!'

"Maybe I am over reacting. I am twenty-one, a woman, and certainly don't want to appear foolish on my birthday." She accepted the logic of her own explanation and said nothing.

"Follow me. You know...I don't like strangers coming into my home, but I can't let you stand outside on a night like this. Ain't fittin' for cats, nor dogs. Follow me," she repeated, leading the way; a tone of animosity underscored her voice. The couple followed quickly behind the woman.

"There is an empty bedroom where you two can stay. This bedroom used to belong to my son and his wife," she continued, walking from the doorway through a hallway; its walls replete with many faded and near faded photographs and portraits of men, women, and children historically garbed; the earliest, British colonial; the latest, a handsome young mustachioed patched-eye army captain, World War II vintage.

The oversized living room housed a large array of antiquated furniture spanning three centuries. An enormous candlelight crystal chandelier suspended by a large tarnished brass chain hung perilously from the ceiling, illuminating a huge collection of valuable oil paintings and exotic tapestries.

From an elaborately ornamented fireplace, ensconced in the corner, glowed a fire of crimson hued logs reflecting a large grandfather clock standing majestically against the adjoining wall, tolling the eleventh hour; its deep tones filling the room.

A hutch on the opposite wall displayed an assortment of pewter, crystal, ceramic pieces, and bone china.

A worn, patched red rug covered the entire floor and continued up the worn oak banister staircase curving to the second floor.

The woman rambled incessantly, pausing periodically to take a deep breath. "The bedroom used to belong to my son. A few years after he turned twenty-five, he married a beautiful twenty-one year old girl. Shortly after their first anniversary, she was killed in an unfortunate accident. My son became so depressed he killed himself that same night."

Her voice softened, a touch of grief swept over her but became severe. Tears rolled down her dated cheeks from gray lusterless sunken eyes hiding behind a pair of small metal rimmed bifocals.

"You are the first people who have been in my house since that time. I hope your short stay will be pleasant."

CHAPTER XI

"My handsome son and my beautiful daughter-in-law went away twenty years ago tonight and have never returned. I wanted grandchildren, but my son and his wife took them away." Anger splintered her voice. "But," she hesitated, "I know they will be back. They will be very sorry they left me. I'll disown them. They won't get any of my money! Why did he kill himself? She wasn't worth it. She was a tramp, I tell you," her voice raised angrily to a fever pitch. She was a tramp...follow me," she repeated gruffly; her feelings had long since been packed on ice and preserved for matters of the mind rather than the heart.

Each step of the stairway painfully illustrated time slowly whittling and eating away at the decaying innards of the old building, for there were as many creaks as there were steps in the ancient stairway.

The wooden banister--richly carved by skilled artisans--was now splintering and rotting. An oriental rug--worn by many years of foot traffic--covered the second story hallway.

"Here is your bedroom," the elderly hostess advised, stopping at a third bedroom.

Melissa noticed the loose fitting door and the two patched small holes in the center; the latch and key plate were different and more modern as compared to the two bedrooms she previously noticed coming down the hallway.

"You can use this bedroom. It belongs to my son and his wife," the woman grunted sardonically.

The word "belongs" caught Melissa by surprise but she said nothing, feeling thankful she and Don would sleep comfortably in a room instead of being cramped up in the bucket seats of his convertible.

"She probably meant 'belonged.' It must have been a slip of the tongue. Old age, loneliness, and suffering have the poor woman very confused." Melissa satisfactorily rationalized the mistake to herself.

"But...we are not married, Mrs._____! Oh, I feel terrible," Melissa stammered then apologized softly; her head slightly bowed. "Please forgive us...We didn't even ask your name."

"Don't matter any," the gray-haired woman snapped. "Taint important what my name is. Tomorrow morning you'll be gone and everything is going to be as before--you are not married?" she asked with some trepidation.

"No," Don emphasized. "We are not, but we plan to be in the near future. Today we were on our way to the Coral Reef, a beautiful nightclub, to celebrate our engagement and Melissa's birthday, but we lost our way. That's how we accidentally arrived at your house. The weather was so bad that we made a wrong turn in the road and couldn't go back. We really feel badly about disturbing you, but we had no other choice. We regret the whole situation," Don concluded apologetically.

The old woman stood, gazing down the hallway, a vacant stare, never blinking an eye, just staring waiting for Don to complete his exhortation.

She cut her silence abruptly, looked at Melissa and spoke in abrupt, weighty, and hollow tones. "All right," she snapped, her voice varied in pitch. "You...what is your name?"

"Melissa, Ma'am...Melissa."

"Melissa you sleep in my son's room and you,...what is your name?" she continued, glancing at Don, her attention centered toward the hallway in some deep expectation.

"What is your name?" She repeated impatiently and impersonally waiting for his answer.

"Don, Ma'am. Don."

"Yes, Don, follow me to the next bedroom. And Melissa, there is a light switch on the wall next to the door. You shouldn't have any difficulty finding it," she advised indifferently.

She ushered Melissa into the room. Then gestured and demanded that Don follow her down the hallway.

The room was large and lofty. Melissa stood at the doorway for a moment, becoming acutely aware of some strange unexplainable apprehension as if there was something ominous.

She groped, found the light switch, and was startled by two black suits of armor, one on either side of the door like wardens guarding the entrance to a dungeon. Abruptly she closed the massive oak door. The broken bolt and missing key gave her an uneasy feeling. There was something about this room she wasn't sure of and it bothered her. Don's muffled voice heard through the wall followed by the slam of a closing door broke her concentration. The thought of his sleeping in the adjoining bedroom eased Melissa's fears.

An electric candelabra and concealed lights revealed the unbelievable as she felt catapulted into the past.

Dark worn draperies partially covered the large windows on one of the walls, while richly engraved oak and teak wood panels adorned the two remaining walls. Handmade mosaics tiled the entire floor. Scattered haphazardly throughout the room were some exotic richly woven oriental and imported rugs. Other rugs were still attached to animal heads, giving the room a medieval air.

The general furniture--an admixture of early French, American colonial, and contemporary--was comfortless and worn. A low golden brocaded divan, several dressing tables with lace doilies, fitted wardrobes, and easy bedroom chairs followed patterns of complete disarrangement.

Near one wall was a heavily hand carved wooden dressing table with a matching chair; a richly decorated French mirror framed in gold leaf hung on the wall above a dresser near the window.

Many books and a few musical instruments lay scattered around. An oversized four-poster black velvet canopied bed hugged the center of the room. Neatly pressed and turned down satin sheets and fluffy down pillows enveloped in matching pillow cases awaited some unknown occupant to rest in their luxury. Nearby a small table stood between a deep armchair and two small chairs.

Two oil portraits--a blonde woman, curiously missing from other portraits of the house; the other, an army captain--crowned by crossed military sabers and a West Point shield hung on the wall beyond the bed.

Melissa walked slowly toward the paintings, being careful not to displace any of the furnishings lest she antagonize her ancient hostess.

Scrutinizing the two portraits, Melissa became fascinated by the officer's tense hand resting on the butt of a pearl handled six-shooter. He wore the pistol openly in a holster strapped to his lean hip like an old gunfighter seemingly ready to withdraw the weapon at a given signal.

"He reminds me of an old cowboy-something out of the past-- an ignoble duplication of a few characters she saw while visiting the wax museum. Maybe as a boy he liked to play with guns and it followed him into adulthood," she joked to herself. This was a time for levity needed to brighten in some small way the otherwise gloomy atmosphere of the room.

Tiredness overcame curiosity.

Upon reaching the bed, she removed Don's jacket and slipped out of her evening dress carefully folding and draping each garment on the back of an easy chair; then she sat on the bed, lifted the sheets, slid under the covers, and covered her tired body.

The cool smooth satin sheets and thin slip pressed comfortably against her figure and she liked it. She relaxed on the cushions; her head resting on one pillow; the other, she noticed, showed varying degrees of discoloration.

An attached light switch on one of the bed posts eliminated the need for using the wall contrivance.

Darkness blanketed the room. Rain, wind, and an occasional clap of thunder continued into the night. Periodically lightning sent quick flashes of light through the glass windows, dispelling the darkness of the room.

A few seconds before Melissa closed her eyes, a faint indistinguishable outline appeared on the window pane and quickly disappeared. "I must be seeing things. Must be the lightning and my imagination playing tricks," she reasoned, burying her face in her hands temporarily then shooting a nervous glance at the window.

Mundane thoughts began disappearing. She finally drifted from reality and sank into a relaxed sleep.

Downstairs the hall clock struck three, suddenly awakening Melissa. Half-drugged, she awoke momentarily.

The heavy pounding of the rain gradually softened as streaks of moonlight broke through the clouds and partially lit the darkened room.

Suddenly a faint garbled conversation exuded from the distance as two figures stood near the half-awakened girl. They were formless, but Melissa knew they had forms concealed from her.

The illusionary beings appeared like luminescent fog that shifts then thickens and thins as it undulates with invisible air currents, projecting salient and misleading hints of their involvement in the past and present. They communicated with looks and gestures more than words, like their souls were intertwined with each other. Unintelligible angry voices filled the room.

CHAPTER XII

The terrorized girl lay motionless frozen by fear. A look of horror swept across her face

All she could see was their size and menace. A shiver ran down her back. Her muscles tensed, paralyzed by the strange fear. Her blood surged frantically through her veins; her pulse beat wildly, and her rapid breathing sounded like wind rushing out of over-inflated balloons.

Cold perspiration covered her forehead and worked its way down her slim body. Her skin rose in bumps of reaction to the apparitions. Her hands became loose and clammy.

She tried to call out but found she had no voice, and the shapeless forms disappeared as quickly as they had appeared. "Was it a nightmare?" she asked herself. "It seemed so real." Reality and the spirit world formed an incongruity in the confused mind of the girl.

Should she run to Don's bedroom and relate what she had experienced. "No." Her decision was firm.

Disturbing her fiancé without surety would be folly and inexcusable. She felt lonely as the uncertainty of the situation gave her an unpleasant feeling precipitated by an aura of confusion.

Relieved, she sank into a deep sleep which calmed the storm that was brewing within her as the night noises and gentle rain became intermingled with her dream voices.

A sudden slap of thunder, hard footsteps, and angry voices filled the bedroom awakening Melissa from a therapeutic dream. A strong fragrance of lilacs pervaded throughout the room.

She sat up, stunned, a frozen statue, shivering and shuddering, galvanized into a state of fear by a terrible realization of impending danger. Her throat tightened. Her chest felt as though it would explode. The rhythm of her breathing increased in frequency. A dizzy terror ran through her mind.

Lightning flashes revealed the former occupants of the bedroom--a young army captain and a tall blonde woman dressed in a hot pink peignoir.

Violent words were exchanged by the couple as they slowly walked past the frightened girl. The captain shot an angry look at his wife. A look of uncertainty filled her tear-laden eyes.

A revolver, the pearl handled one Melissa noticed in the large portrait, was held by the officer, barrel pointed at the woman.

Threats of killing and suicide clearly echoed throughout the room. His words burning with fury.

"But I have no lovers. I never had any affairs with other men. Please believe me! I've always been faithful to you. I only want to be a good wife to you. Please! Please! Don't kill me!" the blonde pleaded, holding a lace handkerchief to her ashen gray disfigured face. Her thin pale lips separated by terror.

"I want a divorce!" she demanded.

"I don't believe you. You are a liar and have been unfaithful. Mother told me that she saw you go out with other men when I was stationed in France. You are no better than a street walker--a damn prostitute. I'd rather see you dead and kill myself then face the men at the camp!"

Denying her pleas, he repeated, "You are no better than a street walker--a damn prostitute! You are a liar...and I hate liars!"

Melissa tried to scream, but her throat went dry, her lips glued shut. She tried to close her eyes fighting to shut out the two spirits as they passed her bed. Each second seemed like hours and it finally ended. The ghostly apparitions disappeared, as quickly as they had appeared.

She was now fully conscious. Cold perspiration covered her face and hands. She raised her hand to her forehead and felt the roots of her hair wet with perspiration.

Her body became temporarily paralyzed. Her uncooperative body remained rooted. With an effort that almost pulled her bones out of their joints, Melissa swung her legs to the floor, threw aside the bed covers and ran, her bare feet hardly touching the rugs, frantically escaping from her chamber of horrors, knocking down a chair on her way out, seeking refuge in Don's room.

The terrified girl's loud impatient staccato knocking echoed throughout the hallway awakening her fiancé. She struggled to find her voice. Finally, after several deep breaths, her words escaped.

"...Don, open up the door... It's me, Melissa. Please let me in!" Crying and out of breath, she repeated urgently, cold tears rolling down her pale cheeks. "It's me, Melissa. Please let me in. Open the door!" she pleaded.

Don abandoned his bed and hastily opened the door. "What is it? What is wrong?" He asked excitedly, embracing the frightened girl, placing her head against his chest. She went limp in his arms.

"It's terrible. It's terrible! The woman's son and his wife....It's terrible!" She spoke incoherently unable to verbally complete her thoughts. She let out a ragged breath.

"Here, Here Let me hold you, you poor darling." Don emphasized sympathetically, cupping her chin with his hand, drawing her lips to his and kissing them tenderly. He wiped the tears from his fiancée's cold face.

The elderly woman appeared shortly thereafter on the scene, wearing a night cap, flannel pajamas covered by a tattered plaid bathrobe tied about the waist with a spotted gray and yellow cord, and confronted the couple.

Don temporarily released Melissa.

"What's all the fuss about? What's the matter?" She inquired quizzically. "Can't a body get some sleep?"

"I saw your son and his wife. They were in my room," Melissa explained hysterically. "He was carrying a gun....and....threatened your daughter-in-law."

"Okay...now, Mel..." Don groped for words. "Tell us the whole thing from the beginning."

The girl, running her tongue over her dry lips, haltingly related the ghostly encounter she had experienced. Her words came out broken, raspy, and terrifyingly vivid.

"Nonsense!" the woman retorted abrasively."My dear son and his wife moved out of this house after he was honorably discharged with the rank of captain from the army at the end of World War II.

"He fought in many battles and was a highly decorated hero. They are now living in Chicago...besides she never used any perfume!"

Melissa curled up in Don's arms like a baby. His strong arms and quiet assurance helped Melissa regain her composure.

Their ancient hostess became hostile and acidly commanded, "Go back to sleep!....you and your nightmare....My son and daughter-in-law indeed. Hmmp! Hah! I'm going back to get some sleep. Young people have such an imagination!" She turned and left, retreating down the long hallway, her voice fading as the distance increased-- "Young people have such an imagination," she repeated, "hmm..." and became silent after slamming her bedroom door.

"O.K., Melissa. You said you saw these two people or ghosts or whatever they were...Did you talk to them? Did they talk to you?"

"No, Don, they passed by my bed but paid no attention to me. They seemed so indifferent to my presence and acted as though I didn't exist. Besides I was too frightened to talk to them. I was in no mood to hold a conversation with a couple of strange spirits."

"Did anything really happen?"

"Not really, Don. But he was pointing a gun at her and was extremely agitated."

"He? You mean the captain?"

"Yes. The captain. The woman's son."

"He threatened his wife? Why?"

"Simply because, his mother said, `she was having affairs with other men and called her a damn prostitute.'" Melissa frowned, feeling uncomfortable repeating the Captain's agitated words.

"What happened to the two spirits?"

"They disappeared! Don, what are we going to do? I am afraid to go back." A note of reluctance was evidenced by her voice.

"Let's go back to your bedroom," he suggested. "I will sit in the hallway near the door. If anything unusual happens, I'll be sitting right there and you can call me. Close the door, but don't lock it..."

"I can't. The key is missing and the bolt is broken," interrupted Melissa.

"Oh, all right. I'll be on guard and make sure no one enters or leaves the room. Let's go. You need your sleep after going through such a harrowing experience."

He held the girl's limp arm firmly and led her to her quarters where he stationed a chair strategically in the hallway.

"This will make a good post. Don't be afraid; I'll be on guard," Don assured her. "I....I'm afraid, Don."

Don felt her tension easing.

She quivered at the thought of entering the darkened room and meeting an unsolicited phantom or two.

He took her into his embrace, soothing her as she apologized profusely for being so emotional and over reacting and kissed the top of her hand.

She crushed his hand and reluctantly released it.

"Don't be afraid, Mel. I'll be out here in case you need me!"

She squeezed her eyes shut and cautiously entered the room, felt for and flipped the wall switch, turning on the lights.

She stood by the doorway, handicapped by fear, looking, glancing, waiting, wandering; her mind reconstructing the appearance and disappearance of the unexpected night visitors; the sight of the unholy couple frozen in her mind.

This unreal experience had been beyond her imagination. Her eyes reached the furthest corners of the room then glanced at the window.

She moved some damp strands of hair from her forehead, drew a long deep breath, picked up the chair, arranged the rumpled garments on it, sat on the edge of the bed for several minutes then slid under the disheveled sheets.

The storm clouds broke into large segmented patches and the moonlight fell in full force where Melissa lay; her eyes and mind seeking relief from the unpleasant and unreal.

Sleep did not come easily. She closed her eyes, but the events of her frightening experience played through her mind like scenes flashing across a movie screen kept her awake. She forced herself to relax, permitting sleep to finally erase her anxieties.

Loud violent threats suddenly interrupted her deep sleep, partially awaking her; she felt totally numb.

The bright moonlight focused on a lone figure, gun in hand, stalking toward the panic-stricken girl.

At close proximity, the girl clearly saw the well-defined features of the military man as clearly as if illuminated by spotlights.

He was an angry man, revengeful in appearance. His small roundish face supported a black heavy mustache, an ugly scar on his right cheek and a dark patch over his left eye. Dark bushy eyebrows, a Romanesque nose with nostrils of unusual formation, well-rounded thin lips and a firmly molded chin gave strength to his features and emphasized his arrogance. His large rounded dark eye cast an eerie glow like a lantern shinning in some deep cavern.

The ghostly white pallor of his skin and dark greasy straight hair parted in the middle glowed in the dark--a countenance not easily forgotten.

Melissa had never seen anyone with such a frightening facade and hoped that she never would again. She lay there, breathless, her heart pounding, fear uncontrollably shaking her body.

The traditional World War II Eisenhower jacket supported several rows of multi-colored decorations; and from each of the captain's shoulders a pair of highly polished silver bars glistened as he moved closer to the girl.

Momentarily he paused at the foot of the bed; his eye darkened ominously narrowing, jerked the pistol out of its holster, leveled the loaded weapon and pointed it at Melissa's head.

Suddenly thoughts of grandmother's stories of murder and suicide, the old lady's lament of her son and his wife, the two portraits on the bedroom wall, the damaged door and the discolored pillow case crazily raced through Melissa's mind like some dismal horror movie.

Enraged, the captain spoke icily, "I finally caught you in bed with your lover!" his voice echoing throughout the partially moonlit chamber.

Melissa's ears were throbbing with pain.

"Now you can't deny it! I'm going to make sure that you will never cheat on me. You tramp....If I can't have you, no one will."

"Captain....I am not your wife. My name is Melissa....you're mistaken!" cried the terrified girl. Her efforts to reason with him were ineffectual. "Please...put the gun down," she pleaded, her mouth drying with each succeeding word.

She closed her eyes as she felt curiously that she wasn't part of an unnatural situation and not actually involved, but a spectator on the sidelines...a spectator of a psychic feeling and not a reality.

"I won't tolerate an unfaithful wife. I'm going to kill you....you tramp....you prostitute...then I'll kill myself!"

He continued, stepping forward with each word until he stood next to the terrified girl, pointing the metal weapon several inches from her forehead. She struggled frantically against the paralysis that immobilized her, facing an inevitable end to her short life.

She clearly saw the index finger curl around the trigger, pressing back slowly. The six-bullet chamber clicked as it revolved, locking the deadly missile in the gun's chamber as the hammer rose in synchronization, waiting for the right signal--like an eager runner--ready to drop and carry out its deadly mission--claim its victim.

The captain stared at her for a moment as though some doubt had crossed his mind, forced the trigger to the back of the revolver, exploding the bullet in the gun's chamber.

CHAPTER XIII

A loud knock at the front door startled Melissa. "Gosh, I must have fallen asleep," yawned Melissa.

She shot a look at her wrist watch, "It's eight o'clock. I guess Don must be working late with a client on an important case. He's very conscientious, hard working, and never late."

She stretched out her arms, and then rubbed her eyes in an attempt to clear her mind. Walking toward the door she caught a glimpse of an old photograph of her grandmother and elderly aunt, a small delicate woman in a toe-length black dress.

Melissa opened the door and screamed; her legs became rubbery; her feet refused to move; she felt faint, and chills ran up her back.

At the entrance stood Don accompanied by a friend--an army captain in his mid-twenties--with a roundish face supporting a thick black mustache, heavy dark eyebrows, and a cloth patch covering one eye. The officer wore an Eisenhower jacket with two rows of multi-colored ribbons and medals, a pair of highly polished silver bars on each shoulder, and a pearl handle six-shooter side-arm housed in a black leather holster strapped to his waist.

###

THE TWO-SIDED BED
By
George Ormond and Riette Suzzette Ormond

"Let's go shopping. We need to buy some groceries and produce," suggested my wife.

"That's a good idea," I agreed. "I'll make a list, and by the way, I want to get the piano bench that we talked about," she reminded me.

"Oh, yeah, I almost forgot. We'll go to the veterans' thrift store where we bought our first piano bench. They have great bargains, and I am sure they'll have one for sale. The other day I went to purchase some old records and saw several piano benches. They were like new. All they needed was a good polishing. I looked around but they didn't have any records. We enjoy polkas, waltzes, vintage music from the '30's, 40's, '50's, Civil War, WWI, and WW II songs. It's great going to the thrift stores for items that are no longer readily available.

We finished breakfast, cleared, washed, dried the dishes, put them away, slipped out of our sleep wear, and dressed.

Soon we were on our way to the grocery store bought our produce, other a sundry items, paid the cashier, and drove to the veteran's thrift store.

Inside the store on the right were long racks of clothing leading to the rear. At the end of the racks was a disarray of assorted furniture pieces and the entrance to a large warehouse that housed hundreds of donated, discarded, and out-dated items including a variety of musical and electronic instruments, furniture, and a mixture of assorted auto parts.

We carefully walked around the irrelevant arrangement and shelves, looking for the piano bench which was partially hidden behind some bedding. We called one of the clerks to please come over and remove the bedding and place the bench in full view.

"Isn't it nice? Just as I told you."

"Yes. It is immaculate," the clerk answered. "It's brand new."

"How much is it," I asked. "Just a minute, I'll ask the manager," he answered and left.

While we were waiting for his answer, we scouted around to find some other useful items. I pointed to a group of shelves where a variety of knick knack's were loosely arranged.

"Hon, I'll look around and see what we can use, and you look around the furniture. Maybe we will be lucky enough to find some valuable antique."

Our exploration began. I went from shelf-to-shelf, inspecting the contents, picking up some items, hoping we could use them but upon further examination realized that nothing fulfilled our needs.

After I finally exhausted my search, I decided to join my wife who came running over very excited. "Sweetheart, you won't believe what I found."

"An old trunk full of gold, silver, and jewels," I kidded.

She grasped my hand and led the way to a pile of wooden and metal pieces of old beds. "Look behind the pile and tell me what you see."

I looked and saw an old brass bed that was partially hidden. "It's just an old brass bed. What's so special about it?"

"Read the metal plate affixed to the side of the right front leg. What does it say?" I got on my hands and knees to read the inscription: "Manufactured by A.C. Simmonds, MDCCCLXIII, for the Lincoln Family, Washington, D.C., Manufacturers of fine beds."

I could hardly believe it. "Do you really want an old brass bed?"

"Yes, yes! My grandmother had a brass bed, and she loved it. The bed reminds me of my happy childhood when grandma held me on her lap. I really want that bed."

I never deny her anything she wants. So if she wants an old bed, she can have it. "O.K. the bed. I don't know where we are going to put it but we'll find a place."

The clerk returned, "The bench is $10." We looked at each other in disbelief that the bench was so inexpensive "And can you drag that old bed out so we can get better look at it?"

"Wow, you don't want an old bed like that. It ain't worth much," the clerk advised while pulling the bed from behind the pile of fragmented beds.

"How much is it?" She asked.

"Hmm, let me see. "

He searched the frame and found a price tag tied to the top runner of the bed. "$50." She was ready to agree to the price, but he continued, "but it is on sale for $15." She agreed with the new price and asked if both items could be delivered to their home.

The clerk summoned the manager and asked him if the items could be delivered.

He faced my wife. "We will be happy to deliver for a small charge of five dollars." He wrote down our name, telephone number, and address. "You live nearby. The merchandise should arrive at your home at no later than five o'clock tomorrow afternoon and thank you very much for your purchase."   We   paid   the   cashier   and   left.

"Can you believe it?" she asked as we drove home.

"No, I can't." That bed must be worth at least $2,000 to $3,000. How much did your grandmother pay for her bed?"

$500, but that was 25 years ago and hers was not an antique."

We arrived at home, and I carried the groceries from the car to the kitchen. The next day we waited for the truck to deliver our prized possessions. The door bell rang at exactly 4:30 P.M.

"Must be the delivery truck!" she exclaimed excitedly. She ran and opened the door. A tall husky man, the girth of a Dallas Cowboy football back, dressed in a pair of Levis, gray shirt, and baseball cap, stood at the door.

"We have an' old brass bed and a piano bench on the truck. Where shall we put it?" he asked in a husky baritone voice. I was standing behind her.

She turned to me and asked, "Where shall we put the bed?"

We were temporarily at a loss because we couldn't decide where to put the bed. She turned and said to the driver, "Please wait, I have to talk to my husband for a couple of minutes."

"Look lady, I have a few more deliveries, and I'll be working past five o'clock my quitting time. So hurry up." His smile suddenly disappeared.

We closed the door, had a quick conference and decided to place the brass bed next to our bed in the bedroom. The one in our bedroom would have to be moved to accommodate our new possession. We opened the door and asked the driver to come in and follow us to our bedroom. He called his partner who looked like a Munchkin out of the Wizard of Oz with a walrus mustache spread across his small thin face and walked with a slight limp. He was balding and a small brown goatee hung from his chin. His white corduroy pants were not pressed and his white shirt was wrinkled. "Come on, Herkimer, the pretty lady needs help."

"I'm coming, Solomon." The pair followed us into the bedroom. "Can you please move this bed to the side of the room then you can bring in the brass bed and place it next to this bed," she asked, pointing to where the new bed would be placed." and the piano bench will go in the living room."

The pair complied. They went to the truck and returned with the springs and brass bed disassembled. They quickly assembled the bed, put the springs on the bed, and went back to their truck. They returned with the piano bench and placed it in the living room.

Before leaving, Solomon handed me a statement and asked me to sign it.

"What is it for," I asked. "So that the D.A.V. knows that I delivered your stuff."

I signed the invoice, handed it to him, thanked the duo, and closed the door after they left.

We inspected the bench for any scratches or breakage. It was as perfect as before. I quickly went to the kitchen, took out the brass cleaner and the can of wax and waxed and buffed the bench to protect the finish.

Cleaning the brass bed was our next project. I carried the brass cleaner from the living room to the bed room. We stood there admiring the Civil War relic and smiled. "Can you believe what a bargain we got?"

"Yes, sweetheart, I still don't believe it."

I pried open the can of brass cleaner, dabbed the contents with one of the cloths that we brought in from the kitchen and handed it to her. I dabbed the other cloth and we both began polishing the frame. We removed the tarnish and the brass metal sparkled. The shined brass reflected our faces.

"It's beautiful," she remarked, admiring their finished product.

We removed the mattress, cushions and sheets from our regular bed and placed them on our new acquisition.

"Let's test it together," and we, simultaneously, laid on the bed. It was very comfortable. I was concerned that we would feel the springs pressing against our backs or that they would be too soft. However my fears were unfounded. The bounce of the springs was perfect--neither too soft nor too hard.

"This is wonderful and so comfortable," she exclaimed. "I can just sleep all day. It's like sleeping on a cloud."

There seemed to be something magical about it but I couldn't explain. We have slept on a lot of beds going cross country from California to Florida but none of them were as comfortable as this one.

"Come on sleepy head we have to make dinner." Reluctantly, we left the bed, cooked, and ate our dinner.

While she was making some booties for our pet goose, I was reading a novel about the Civil War. At about ten o'clock we decided to go sleep. Rain drops began to hit the bedroom window and the rumble of thunder sounded in the distance. The sound of rain lulled us to sleep. We laid on our brass bed, held and kissed each other good night, and quickly fell asleep.

A slap of thunder woke me up; flashes of light entered the window and cut across the room. I looked around and realized that the room was unfamiliar. I looked for a light switch but there was none. On a table, next to the bed, was a candle holder with one candle.

A candelabra with three candles hung from the ceiling. Several Daguerreo types of people, none that I could recognize, covered part of the one wall; the other walls, were blank with a grayish wood finish. Hooked on a wooden hat rack close to the door was a blue Civil War vintage Union general's Civil War military cap with a U.S. army insignia.

Sleeping, next to me, lay a strange woman dressed in a long muslim nightgown and night cap. She looked vaguely familiar but I couldn't place her. She was approximately 5 ' 3" tall, fair complexion, long brown hair, and decidedly good looking. I tried to remember who she was.

After a few seconds I realized that she was Maria Zepe, a Union military fighter, and distant cousin, whose photograph I had seen in my great grandmother's photo album.

I raised myself up from a prone position and sat on the edge of the bed. The flashes of light revealed that I was wearing a Union general's uniform--a double- breasted dark blue embroidered frock coat with two rows of shining gold buttons, gilt-edged shoulder straps with three stars, the middle star larger than the outer two metallic gold stars, one on each of my shoulders, epaulets, a sash and numerous medals pinned across my chest, blue trousers with a gold stripe extending from my hips to the bottom of each leg, Jefferson boots, a gold-plated handle sword within its leather scabbard attached to my black waist leather belt, extending almost the full length of my right leg and an empty pistol holster on my left side. A pair of embroidered gloves and a sabretasche filled with maps and confidential papers lay next to me on my right side. From a mirror across the room I saw that a black heavy beard and mustache covered my face, and my black hair trailed down to my shoulders.

I bent down and saw the same identical metal plate in the same location as the shiny bed where I had initially fallen asleep. A chamber pot was near the right rear leg. The sound of thunder and lightning increased in intensity. I sat up.

The sleeping girl woke up. "What are you doing here?" she asked. "You are supposed to be out there with your army unit fighting the Confederates."

"How did I get here?" I asked incredulously.

"What do you mean 'how did I get here?' You and General Meade are in command of the Union forces defending **Chancellorville** against the Confederate Generals Lee and Jackson." She picked up a flint stone, scratched it, and lit the candle. The candle light showed how pretty she was.

"I am not a general. All I ever was a corporal in the war." I advised her. But she wouldn't listen.

"Get out there and defend **Chancellorsville** against the Confederates. Don't be a coward," she admonished.

"But I don't know anything about fighting a war," I responded.

"Get out and fight the 'rebs and stop your complaining!" she responded, raising her voice and from under her pillow she brought out and pointed at my head a Colt '44.

I was caught off guard and didn't know what to do.

She lowered the weapon and handed it to me, repeating, "Don't be a coward, take this pistol, fight the rebs' and stop complaining. Abe gave you three stars, now do something with them."

"I took the weapon and slid it into the empty gun holster.

"Tell me how this bed got here?" I .asked.

"You have a war to fight, men are being killed, and you ask me about a bed!?" she angrily screamed.

"Yes. It is important to me."

"Well, the bed was manufactured in Pennsylvania and was shipped with other pieces of furniture. The furniture shipment was secretly being shipped to Washington, D.C. for President Lincoln 's wife. Everything was handmade. Somehow a group of Rebs got past the front line in a little known trail and intercepted the freight coach. They killed the driver and the horses, destroyed the furniture, burned the coach but saved the bed and brought it down to this deserted farm house. I was hiding in the bushes when they entered the house, carrying the disassembled parts."

I quietly left the bushes being careful not to be seen, looked inside through a window and saw two of the men putting the parts together. I recognized one of the men as a former captain in the Union army who was dishonorably discharged for selling military secrets to the South. Before they were finished, I ran to the bushes and watched the two men mount.

"Joshua, we can use the bed after we win the war," one of the men advised as the group headed South.

She hesitated for a few seconds and said, "Now, go out there and help win the war against the Rebs'."

I thanked her for the information and left.

I quickly got up and picked up my hat on the way out. The sounds of heavy artillery, horses galloping, troops yelling, and rifle fire filled the atmosphere. A white horse was fully saddled and ready for my departure. I mounted the animal and joined General Meade's troops. From a small hill I had a full view of the two opposing armies.

The carnage was horrendous. "Americans killing Americans. What a waste of humanity. and all for a few stupid principles that should have been amicably settled," I thought to myself as I saw rows upon rows of men, like toy soldiers, killed or wounded at the crack of rifles and roar of cannons.

I joined General Meade at his headquarters, a makeshift tent with a table and some chairs, occupied by Brigadier General George Getty, General Thomas Neil, Brigadier General John Wheaton, Colonel Lewis Grant, Brigadier General Henry Eustis, and General Meade sitting at the table.

I conferred with him and suggested flanking the Rebs' and then encircling them. He said that would weaken the front line and a frontal attack would be the best strategy. Reluctantly, I agreed, left him and joined the VI corps, 2nd division in a frontal attack.

The battle was fierce. There were regular sheets of flame from rows of leveled rifles. Around and in front of me Union soldiers were dropping, dead or wounded on the spot as the opposing army aimed and fired their rifles and cannons. The rifle balls and bullets--54 caliber minnie balls, .52 metallic cartridges, and .58 explosive bullets-- filled the sky like confetti during a parade.

Men screamed in pain as the rifle balls hit their targets; as blood ran like rivulets out of their bodies, others stopped for a few seconds and dropped to the ground, legs and arms and heads violently amputated. I removed my sword from its sheath and parried two bayonet thrusts, accidentally cut the arm of a Reb soldier. I removed my colt '44 from its holster and shot two soldiers, each one in the right foot. I didn't want to kill anyone. Cannon balls were mowing Federal soldiers, like pins in a bowling alley, instantly killing and wounding several hundred men simultaneously.

Suddenly I felt a sharp pain. A ball had hit my shoulder and it was bleeding profusely. I held on tight to my horse and returned to the farm house.

Lee and Jackson split their army, outflanked and drove us back across the Rappahannock River with substantial losses. The South won with more than 10,000 casualties.

Maria met me at the front of the farm house. The bleeding had weakened me so much that I was leaning to one side causing me to fall sideways. She ran to my aide catching me as I was falling off the horse. She carried me in, placed me on the bed, and took off my blood soaked coat and shirt. Then with a wet cloth, she swabbed my injured shoulder and compressed the wound to stop the bleeding. "You are lucky. The rifle ball went clear through otherwise you would be dead by now.

And how did the battle go?"

"We regretfully had to retreat," I answered. "My shoulder is very painful," I complained. She left me for a few minutes and came back with a bottle of homemade liquor.

"Here drink this," she demanded. "It won't cure you but it will put you to sleep."

I drank almost half the bottle. The liquor was so strong that my mouth felt as though it was on fire (I had never drunk a beverage stronger than apple cider). I fell asleep. While I was sleeping, Maria poured some of the whisky on my injured shoulder and washed it. Then she got a needle, a spool of thread, and sewed together my shoulder wound.

I was delirious for several days. When I was lucid, Maria would ask, "What is car? And what is an airplane? What are Nazis? And who is Mrs....?"

I tried to answer but fell asleep. Evidently, I talked in my sleep. She took very good care of me: feeding, bathing, and shaving me.   She would wash the bed sheets and change them when possible. Soap was very scarce but she knew where to get it. For food she would go out and come back with a variety of small animals she trapped and shot in the woods. She was an expert marksman with a rifle and a pistol. The meat was made into a tasty stew and the fur into clothing.

On the fourth day my wound was healing nicely and the pain had lessened to a tolerable degree. I sat on the bed fully awake and she asked me the same questions.

I answered all her questions but she found it hard to believe.

"You look very handsome without all those whiskers," she would add.

That night I fell asleep with Maria keeping vigil just as she had for three days. I believe that she was falling in love with me. I could tell from the way she looked at me.

I opened my eyes the next day. I was lying on the brass bed with my wife sleeping next to me. She woke up and we looked at each other. "I am back home," I exclaimed.

"You have been here all the time except something strange happened that I can't explain. For a couple of seconds a strange man appeared then disappeared. He had on a Civil War general's uniform. I don't know where he came from or how he got here."

I breathed a sigh of relief to be home with my wife in our bed. She looked at my shoulder and asked,   "Where did you get that small red mark on your shoulder?"

"I don't know," I lied.   "I must have hit myself by accident."

A few days later, we visited the veteran's thrift store. I reached onto one of the shelves and picked up an old Civil War photograph. We were amazed with what we saw: a picture of Maria and me. She, sitting on a chair, and I, clean shaven, lying in bed with a bandage around my shoulder.

###

THE REVOLVING DOOR--A TIME FOR CHANGE©

By

Riette Suzzette Ormond
And
George Ormond

George Lincoln Wardsworth, a descendant of Abraham Lincoln, proudly fondled his Ph.D. awarded to him at his graduation by one of the Harvard University faculty members,

He was an outstanding high school athlete --big enough to play football, basketball (6' 2", 160 pounds) and baseball. He was an outstanding scholar, maintaining an A+ grade point, he graduated Summa Cum Lauda, was president of the senior class; and as valedictorian was invited to make the graduation speech

Five top universities offered him four-year-scholarships. He chose Harvard. His majors: archaeology to learn the social evolution of people; psychology to understand thinking processes, economics to analyze the economy, and journalism and advertising how to present new products to the public.

He maintained a 4.0 average, was invited to join an honorary fraternity, received a Phi Beta Key, wrote numerous articles for the Harvard Law Review, school newspaper, and magazine. George excelled in sports, received a number of awards, and met and became engaged to Sally, a beautiful coed.

For employment, he solicited   Meyers, Drew, and O'Brian, an outstanding old line advertising agency--one of the top rated advertising firms in New York City. After reading George's resume and letters of commendations, the interviewer hired George immediately at $100,000 a month; his title, vice-president in charge of advertising media, (his job--devise advertising methods which will improve product presentation and increase corporation sales).

He presented his first idea to the board: Place a band on the roof of the building, a man dressed in black, and an almost invisible rope. The man slides down the rope, drops down 10 floors waving a large banner with the name of the company and product while the band plays the national anthem. All the radio and television stations would be invited to participate and advertise the event.

Some of the members saw it as a dangerous production, but the majority agreed that it had a great deal of merit and voted to carry out the plan.

The media publicized the event to be staged the following Tuesday, 12:00 noon in front of the building. At the designated time, the band members sat on the roof and waited for a large crowd to gather at the base of the building. Their attention to be focused on the top of the building, waiting for the band to start playing, and the man to drop down 20 stories with a large banner the size of the skyscraper.

The band began to play; the man draped himself in the banner, stepped to the edge of the roof and jumped. Some of the crowd gasped and others began shouting: "He's gonna be killed. Where is the rope to hold him? Look at that stupid guy jumping without a parachute or a rope! What the hell are those people thinking of they are killing a guy to make a few bucks--that's disgusting!"

On his descent, the man opened the banner with the message: "Eat YUBBIES for your health specially formulated. for muscle build-up and energy increase--Guaranteed." His descent ended abruptly on the 10th floor. The audience felt relieved, applauded, and dispersed.

The YUBBIE Company president was ecstatic and called George, practically screaming, "Congratulations! That was a brilliant show. Our sales have increased dramatically over 50%. You people are geniuses. Thank you very much."

George Lincoln proposed similar advertising shows using: Niagara Falls, the Grand Canyon, and other important sites throughout the world. The results were outstanding. Sales increased on the average 40 to 60%. He was promoted to general control of all media advertising.

The Sweetser Candy Company contracted with George's company to advertise a new drink. He was assigned to make a commercial aimed at ten-year- olds. The subject: a drink to please that age bracket, and after several days, he devised a commercial aimed at that age group.

George presented the commercial to the board that they approved. The idea: go to a park and choose the highest slide.   A ten-year old climbs up carrying a cup of Chikbleu, the company's latest health drink: a blend of chocolate, milk, blueberries, vitamins, and amino acids.

One child slides down as another child climbs to the top while holding a cup of Chikbleu. The first child stops half-way (a hidden wire holds him in place) waiting for the second child to slide down and meet him. When they meet each other, (the wire releases) both youngsters slide down, sit with their parents, and hold up their cups of Chickbleu.

A voice announces: "Drink Chikbleu for health, vigor, and energy in the morning with your breakfast, at night before going to bed, and you will feel very refreshed and invigorated when you wake up the next morning. Chikbleu is a very pleasant, tasty smooth beverage;   you drink your vitamins instead of swallowing them whole.

"Chikbleu is a combination of rich dark chocolate, whole enriched milk, fresh blueberries, and the FDA recommended top quality vitamins. No salt, sugar or preservatives have been added. Once you drink Chickbleu, you will never again drink another beverage. So drink Chikbleu for health and enjoyment!"

At this point in the background, a fairy godmother appears, drinking a cup of Chikbleu (Chikbleu is inscribed on the cup, in upper case letters) and she announces: "Chikbleu helps me to fly. I would never be without it," and fades away.

The family drinks Chikbleu, saying, "This is a very tasty drink. We drink two cups of Chikbleu every day--morning and night."

The board approved the commercial, signed a contract with the television station and it aired on television for ten months. The Sweetster Candy Company experienced an 80% rise in sales. The treasurer of the company telephoned and said, "Hya., this is Harold Schwarts, treasurer of the Sweetster Candy Company. You people are magicians. We love you! You are great. Our sales jumped 80% this month. I want to thank you. You will always be our 'ad' company.

"Six months from now we plan to sponsor a contest and we want you in charge."

The board congratulated George, gave him a raise and a bonus. He enjoyed the praise more than the money. From his cell phone he called Mike, the parking valet, and advised him that he was leaving and to have his car at the front He left the board room and returned to his office, picked up his brief case, walked out of his office, rode the elevator down to the lobby, and left the building through the revolving door, The parking valet was in front with his car. George said, "Thank you Mike, have a good night," got in his car and drove home.

The drive home was very boring; the traffic, tiresome. To avoid going to sleep, he played musical CD's and sang. He remembered the commercial he had just finished and wondered, "What would it be like being a ten-year old again?" and dismissed it.

He arrived at his home, opened the automatic car garage door, drove into the garage, parked, and entered the house through a rear door.

He was greeted by the maid who offered him a sandwich and coffee. Having finished his snack, he said, "Good night to the maid," and went to bed.

He lay in bed remembering his tenth birthday. There was no "happy birthday, no congratulations, nor a birthday cake."

His father would come home late, broke, his pay check taken from him by the gambling tables and his "friends' the dice." His anger would chase George out of the house for several hours. Food was scarce and George was forced, by hunger, to get some part jobs to feed the family of four. He despised his home and found refuge in his studies at Roosevelt middle school.

He was loved by the majority of his peers, his being kind, intelligent, understanding, and helpful. He helped anyone who needed assistance with any subject. During lunch time, students enjoyed sharing their lunch with him. The student body said he was more intelligent than the faculty, including the school principal.

The principal., sunken cheeks, enormous indented dark round eyes, six feet tall, horned rimmed thick glasses, and lanky was dubbed by the student body as the "Halloween face" or "skin and bones" He was always somber; never smiled nor had a kind word, was disliked by both the students and faculty alike.

The teachers loved George, said that he was very intelligent and had a keen sense of humor. In the classroom when the teacher busied herself filling the blackboard with boring subject matter to "educate the students" (a cliché' used by the teachers) whether they liked it or not. George would mimic or make jokes about the principal or some other teacher and the class would explode with laughter. The laughter pleased the teacher. She assumed that the joke she had composed and presented to the class created such an outstanding reaction. She would turn around and thank the students. The passing bell would ring and the class was dismissed.

When all the students went home, George would remain after school with a teacher on a pretext of needing help with some subject matter. When the teacher went home, he left school. He finally dosed off and sleep erased his memories.

He awoke early, showered, shaved, dressed, and ate a hearty breakfast of bacon, eggs, sunny side up, coffee, toast, and marmalade.

He addressed his maid, "Daisy, don't wait up for me. I'll be working late."

"Very good, I won't wait. I'll call if there are any important calls."

He put on his hat and left.

Driving down the street, he looked in the rear view mirror and saw behind him a flashing red light. He pulled over to the curb and waited.

A policeman approached and faced him.

"Officer, what is wrong?"

"One of your tail lights is out. Please take care of it as soon as possible."

"Thank you, officer. I will."

The officer mounted his motorcycle and left.

George continued driving to his office. On the way he once again wondered what it would be like if he were ten years old.

He called the parking valet to meet him in front of the building. The valet was waiting in front, George stopped, slid out, was replaced by the valet who parked the car.

George walked toward and entered the building's revolving door. Of the four spaces, he occupied one; three women, the other three.

The door began revolving but suddenly halfway through it stopped. George attempted to push it but the door seemed stuck in place. He pushed with all his strength, but the door remained firm.

He looked outside the glass enclosure and was puzzled, The tall buildings had disappeared and a row of one story modest homes, one white with yellow trim, another pink with brown trim, all with manicured lawns, and a small picket fence; built circa 1964 by obviously the same builder, paralleled the street.

A distance away, barely visible, was an oil derrick with a large sign CHICKASAW OIL COMPANY. He couldn't believe it. He was back in the town he left fifteen years earlier when he entered the University.

Chikasaw, Oklahoma, had been a booming oil town during the 1930's with five derricks pumping petroleum at full speed, however the demand for oil diminished and four of the five derricks were dismantled.

Suddenly, the glass enclosure automatically opened and then quickly disappeared. He found himself on the steps of an old hotel constructed in 1893. The structure had been condemned but the towns people refused to have it razed.

The three people in the revolving door, the office building where he worked, and the door had vanished. He walked forward, splintering a floor board, almost falling into a cellar, three stories below. He pulled himsel up out of the broken floor board and saw a reflection in a half broken mirror nearby on the floor. He picked up the mirror and couldn't believe what he saw--the reflection of a ten-year boy--he continued starring in disbelief.

How could this be? What had happened? He didn't remember changing clothes. He had entered the revolving door as a man and even when the door jammed, he was still a man. Once again he looked in the mirror; nothing had changed since he stared at himself moments before. However, he was now a child and his clothing fit.

It was as though when he became smaller, his clothing also shrunk. He kept asking himself, "How could that be?" His mental processes continued to function the same as before the physical change. Mentally he was still a man; physically, a child. He continually appraised the situation while deciding what to do.

He was now a child and could do nothing to change it, therefore he decided to go to his former home and stay with his family, but, first he wanted to visit some of the neighbors. His home, located at 1244 Lincoln Avenue--two blocks from the old hotel. . .

He knocked on 1200 Lincoln where he often had baby sat with Mrs. Cavanugh's 2-year old twins. A pretty petite blonde teen-ager in Levis and a short sleeved white blouse, answered the door.

"Yes? What can I do for you?" Her greeting was nonchalant and rather indifferent.

"It's me. George Lincoln Wardsworth. I live down the street in the next block and baby sat with Shirley and Shirey.

"Just a minute, " she interrupted. "I'll get my mother." She closed the door part way and called her, "Mother..."

"Yes, Jackie, what is it?"

"There is a strange boy at the door. Are you coming down?"

"Yes, I am putting on something. I'll be there shortly."

The girl opened the door and faced George.

She became more attentive and asked, "What is your name?"

Somewhat vexed, he answered, "I told you George Lincoln Wardsworth."

"You are kidding. Is that your real name?"

"Of course it is. I live a block away down the street. Don't you remember me?"

"No, I don't remember you."

The mother joined the twosome, interrupted the conversation and asked "Little boy, who are you?"

He explained who he was, lived down the block, baby sitting with the twins. and the delicious breakfast she cooked. Suddenly her two adorable blonde twins came to the door and hugged their mother's legs.

"I'm sorry I don't remember you, little boy. You'll have to excuse me. I have to be at work in half an hour," she said as she picked up the twins and left.

The girl remained for a short time and, with a twinkle in her eyes, invited him. "You are welcome to visit us anytime."

"Thank you, but I don't have the time," he responded.

A disappointed look crossed her face as she entered the house and closed the door.

He knocked on the door of the adjoining house. He always liked Mrs. Goldberg. She had no children and "adopted" him. Her husband and son had been killed in a car accident several years ago and she was lonely. She would invite him to join her and celebrate Rosh Hashanah, Passover, and Yom Kippur. Her Jewish foods: matzos, gefilte fish, matzo gebrach, chicken soup with matzo balls, chopped liver, kneidles, lox, white fish, halavah, and other courses, were delicious

A short chunky gray haired woman answered the door. "Nu, vat is it?"

She looked at George and asked, "Boychik, Vat can I du for you?"

"Mrs. Goldberg, don't you know me? You invited me to eat dinner and celebrate the Jewish holidays. I live in the next block, down the street,"

"Vat ist yor name, boychik?"

"George Lincoln Wadsworth. You always said that my great grandfather, Abraham Lincoln, was Jewish."

"Ver du yu lif, liddle boi?"

"Next block, down the street." he repeated and pointed in that direction

She became pensive and finally answered, "I am sorry, boychik, I don't rememba. Maybe if you came some odder times, maybe I will rememba. Gud bye and lots of lock, liddle boi," she said, closing the door .behind her. .

He knocked on the Silver's home. Mr. Silver, a strikingly handsome blond man, gray temples, in his mid-to-late 50's dressed in a black turtleneck sweater and black slacks, answered the door.

He called his wife and she came to the front door, wearing pearl earrings and a cotton print dress.

She addressed the boy, smiled and asked, "Honey, what can we do for you?"

He repeated his name and address, however she was unresponsive.

"No sweetheart, we don't know who you are. We didn't know that the Wardsworth had a son. That's news to us." She looked at her watch and reacted somewhat alarmed. Its 8:30! We are late. You'll have to excuse us; we have to get to work."

"But don't you remember, I used to swim in your swimming pool."

"We never had or have a swimming pool. Now if you'll excuse us, we have to get to work," she repeated.

The couple opened the garage door, got in the car, and drove off, automatically closing the garage door.

He couldn't understand what was happening, he thought to himself, and walked toward the next house.

1206 Lincoln Avenue, home of the Colombia residence. It was believed by the town residents that the Colombia's were descendants of Columbus. The story, (which was never substantiated) it seems, was that when Christopher Columbus came to America, he co-habitated with an Indian princess. The princess gave birth to twins; one was a male; the other, a female. It was from the male offspring that the Colombia family descended. The townspeople treated the family like royalty, and every year the residents celebrated Columbia day.

He remembered the lavish "Cinco de Mayo" parties the Colombia family staged. On long tables covered with embroidered damask table cloths, large silver platters were laden with an enormous variety of Mexican food: tacos, enchiladas, frijoles, fried arroz (rice), chicharrones de puerco, guacamole, pan (bread), tortillas--corn and flour--tortilla chips, barbecued chickens,   beef, pork and every beverage, wine and liquor devised by man.

The family income was derived from a diamond mine in South Africa, two gold mines in South America, an oil derrick, and could well afford the expense.   Neighbors, friends, and relatives were all invited to the celebration.   The family enjoys watching people have a good time.

George's family was usually invited.   The food was delicious and he ate some of each until he was satisfied.   He also remembered that in the Mexican family there were the parents and four sons: Sancho, Pancho, Pedro, and Pepe--ages 2 to 12.

He knocked on their door and waited.   A lady, in her late 20's holding a toddler, opened the door.

"Muchachito, what can I do for you?" she asked cordially.

George repeated his name and address and that he lived in the next block, and continued, "What a cute baby. Is it a boy or a girl? How old is the baby? What is the baby's name?"

"The baby is a girl, four months old, and her name is Genevieve. Now what can I do for you, muchachito? "

He asked her if she remembered him baby sitting with her four sons and the wonderful breakfast of huevos ranchero, hot flour tortillas, garlic Mexican toasted bread, toasted bread brimming with strawberry marmalade, and that delicious sweet Mexican chocolate she served him as payment for his baby sitting service.

It was almost noon; he was hungry and hoped that Mrs. Colombia would invite him to share a delicious dinner with her family.

She looked at him and responded, "Muchachito (she called anyone under 12 years old, muchachito--- little boy'), I am sorry but I don't remember you. Maybe you made a mistake and live someplace else in the city. I didn't know that the Wardsworth family had a son.

"Un minuto'" she began speaking in Spanish-- "por favor. I'll call my husband, Papa! Papa!"

"Si, Margarita, que quieres?" (Yes, Margarita, what do you want)?

"Vengase por favor. Te necesita."(Please come here, I need you).

A short man, 5' 4", dark hair, sun tanned, sporting a thick black mustache, carrying a saw, responded to his wife's call.

"Si Margarita, que pasa? (Yes,.Margaeita,what's happening?)

" Jose, Este muchachito esta preguntando si ya le consco (Jose, this little boy is asking if I recognize him)."

"Bueno le conosas? (Well, do you recognize him?)

"No, Jose, I usted?" . she asked. (No, Jose, do you?)

"Nunca le vio y yo no conosco el muchachito. (I never saw him and I don't recognize the little boy)," he answered.

"El esta diciendo que el es un hijo de la familia Wardsworth (He is saying that he is a son of the Wardsworth family)," she answered, pointing down the street.
"Creo que es una mentira, Margarita. La Senora Wardsworth nunca tenia hijos (I think that's a lie, Margarita, Mrs. Wardsworth never had any sons.)."

"I am sorry, chikito, but we don't remember you, maybe you live in another part of the city. I am sorry , muchachito, we don't remember you, we don't know who you are, and Mrs. Wardsworth never had a son You'll have to excuse us," she said politely, "I have to feed my baby and cook dinner for my family, I hope you find what you are looking for. Good bye and good luck."

They closed the door, leaving George bewildered. He remained on the porch several minutes then remembered a grocery store, where he used to shop, was about four blocks away.

"This is the second time I've been told that I never existed I'll go to the grocery store and buy a few things for my family before I visit them. The store clerks will remember me." The store was on Roosevelt Boulevard.

He reached into his rear pocket where he kept his wallet containing three hundred dollars, driver's license, and credit cards but it was all gone. His other pockets were also empty. He searched his pockets several times but all his money, car keys, a few coins, a small picture of his fiancée, his cell phone and a handkerchief had all disappeared.

He began walking as rain clouds obscured the sun. and a storm quickly developed. Hail, moth ball size, pelted his face, large droplets of rain began drenching his clothes, and a strong cold wind whipped around him George ran and sought refuge in a bank a fourth of a block away.

A bank robbery was in process. Two men holding automatic weapons were giving orders to the personnel. On the floor, lying prone, face down, were two men and one woman. A pool of blood surrounded one man.

"All right, If you don't do as I tell you, you'll get the same as your bank cashier," one of the robbers threatened the manager, pointing the muzzle of the gun at his temple.

The other one stood guard over the rest of the employees to avoid any difficulty that might arise.

The police arrived, surrounded the building and shouted a warning to the robbers, "Come out with your hands up, throw out your guns. If you don't come out in five minutes, we are coming in shooting!"

"Listen, copper, we aren't coming out in five minutes or five days."   .

In the rear of the building, A small window, covered with a screen and partially broken glass, was used by the police to enter the bank. A petite police woman quietly cut the screen, carefully removed the glass, and entered the room. She crawled slowly over to George, shielded him and held her hand over his mouth to avoid his alerting the criminals and pointed her gun at the other.

The one robber, becoming aware of the officer's presence, turned around and shot. Two bullets pierced the police woman's chest, saving George's life. The wounded officer quickly reached out, knocked the gun out of the bank robber's hand, and instantly returned the gunfire killing both bank robbers as they fell to the floor. The rest of the policemen rushed into the bank.

Shortly thereafter, several ambulances arrived and carried the wounded and dead to the nearest hospital.

While the police woman was being carried out by the medics, George walked next to her stroking her long blond hair, patting her creamy skin, and looking at her brilliant blue eyes,

Her red lips partially parted trying to speak, she looked up and saw him, than her eyes closed and she became silent.

Tears flowed down his checks as he walked next to her until she was placed inside the ambulance, repeating, "Thank you for saving my life, thank you, thank you."

One of the policemen gently put his arm on George's shoulder and urged him to leave the bank. "Son, there is nothing you can do."

"Officer, I want to thank you and everybody for coming.

Good bye."

"Good bye, son."

The storm had passed and the sun lit the sky. "Boy, this is one chapter in my life I'll never forget. Thanks to that brave police woman I am alive. I pray she survives," he thought to himself.

He arrived at the store and walked over to Clarrissa, the store manager. She was statuesque 5 feet 9 inches tall, long shoulder length red hair with blond streaks radiating from the center of her head, smooth creamy white skin, ruby red lips, blue eyes, well-proportioned body, wearing a cotton dress two inches above her knees, busy stocking shelves.

Previously, George would tell her that he had lost the money his mother had given him to buy some groceries and asked if she would give him some cans, and he would pay her back when his mother gave him more money. She knew that his family was very poor, would give him the groceries, and pay for the items.

Although she was ten years older than George, they were good friends. He often told her, "When I grow up, I am going to marry you, I promise."

"O.K. buster. When you are my age, I'll marry you. I promise," she would answer humorously. Like a mother, she always took care of him.

"Hello, Clarissa ...," She interrupted him "What do you want, kid?" She asked sarcastically.

"Don't you remember me? I'm George Lincoln Wardsworth. I live on Lincoln Avenue."

"I don't remember you and I don't know who you are. Now what do you want, kid?"

"I want to buy some groceries for my family but I don't have any money. I'll pay you back later."

"Use your credit card," she suggested, pointing to the credit card swiping machine.

"I don't have a credit card. I am not old enough to have a credit card."

"How old are you?"

"Ten years old."

"That's right, I forgot. They don't issue credit cards if you are under the 16 age limit and then you have to get permission from your parents."

She motioned to one of the clerks and said, "Give this kid two cans of soup and some slices of salami and six slices of bread. He looks hungry."

One of the clerks remarked, "Clarissa, you are a soft touch. I too felt sorry for the kid."

George thanked the manager and the clerk and left the store. He hadn't eaten since breakfast. He sat on a wrought iron chair, placed the bag with the cans of soup on his lap, made three sandwiches and hungrily ate them. The clerk had placed the cans of soup in a paper bag. He picked up the bag and decided to surprise his family.

Arriving at 1220 Lincoln, he rang the door bell. While waiting, he looked around, something was missing, the quaint doll house on the sunny side, where he and his sister enjoyed playing house. Now the small area where the doll house had stood was overrun with wild grass and weeds, whereas previously the area next to the house had been dotted with neat rows of rose bushes and flowers.

"Yes, what is it," came a muffled female voice from the interior of the house.

"It's me, George."

"We don't know anybody named George. George who...?"

"Your brother George. Don't you remember me?"

"I don't have a brother," she said from behind the door. Finally, the door opened and a 12- year-old, stepped onto the porch.

"Cecila, don't you know who I am?"

"Who are you? Never had a brother... Mother!" she shouted. "Mother," she repeated.

A faint voice answered, "Just a minute, I'll be there in a few minutes."

A few minutes later a 5'2"petite brunette in her early 30's stepped out of the house and joined the two youngsters.

"What is it? What's the... Who are you, young man?" She looked at him quizzically.

"Mother, this kid says he is my brother is that true? You never told me about it."

"Of course not Cecilia, you never had a brother. Tell me young fellow, where did you get the notion that we are your parents?"

"What happened to the doll house where Ceclia and I used to play?" he asked, pointing to the empty spot where the doll house had been located.

"Some of the neighborhood kids got into it, had some candles, lit a match, the curtains caught on fire, and it burned down," the mother explained.

He continued, "Do you remember when I tied a steak to our dog because I wanted to see tiger go round and around trying to catch the steak?"

"And when dad and I were riding on the ferris wheel, I almost fell and dad caught me when we were on top because I wanted to touch a cloud. And on the farm we visited, I took dad's belt and started to drop it down the outhouse hole to see how far it was going to go.

"Luckily dad was there and caught me because I would have fallen into the hole. And when I lit a match and burned the bathing suits because they had ants and I wanted to get rid of the ants?"

He looked around but his father was nowhere in sight. "Where is dad?"

"Dad, as you call my husband, is in the hospital."

"What happened?"

"Maybe you know, he is the maintenance man on the oil derrick. While he was fixing some gear or something like that at the bottom of the tower, a careless workman working on the top dropped a heavy wrench and broke my husband's arm."

"How bad is it?"

"His arm was broken in three places, and it's going to take three months before it will be completely healed. I don't know what we are going to do for money."

"I have two cans of soup you can have."

The girl gratefully accepted the cans, carried them into the house, returned, and joined her mother.

"Now young man, what can I do for you?"

"Mom, I need a place to stay."

"I am not your mother and we don't invite strangers to live with us."

"But I am not a stranger, I am your son," he pleaded.

"You'll have to find another place to stay.   Come along Cecilia."

The woman reached out, pulled the girl by her hand, entered the house, and closed the door.

"Now what am I going to do.?" the boy asked himself.   "I know. I'll go to my school. They will remember me."

Five blocks later, he arrived at the main gate of his school. The teacher on guard was temporarily distracted by a student and George walked through the gate. It was recess time and the students were enjoying themselves running, playing games and some were screaming.

He walked over to a small group of his friends playing marbles and joined them. He was unnoticed by the boys. "Hya Mark," he said. The boy did not respond.

"Hey, Mike it's me."

Again, there was no response. "It's me, George.   Isaac , Melvin, don't you remember me--your friend?"   .

"If you don't go away, we'll call a teacher! " Melvin warned him and continued playing.

Disgusted, he saw five girls who always enjoyed eating lunch with him, jumping rope. "Hya, Dora, it's me, George."

The girls looked at him, said nothing, and continued with the game.

He addressed Betty Jane, Claudia, Markeeta, Yvonne, and Josephina who paid no attention and continued playing. Josephina left the group and returned with a teacher.

"That strange boy is bothering us," she advised the woman who sternly warned him that if he didn't leave the girls alone, she would report him to the principal.

Not wanting any trouble, he began to mingle with the rest of the students. Suddenly one of the students grabbed George by his shoulder and pushed him to the ground. Surprised, he raised himself up and faced the student . He recognized the boy. It was "Butch" Larkin, a year older and a head taller, who with four companions had a bad reputation as bullies picking fights, taking younger children's lunches, and demanding "protective" payment from others . George previously had some difficulties with "Butch."

"I saw you making faces at Freida, my girl friend. Keep away from her. Do you understand? If you don't, I'll punch your face in!"

Before he could respond, "Butch" began hitting George with his closed fists.

George returned the punches, knocking the older boy to the ground.

Students began grouping around the two gladiators, shouting, "Common, hit him again! Hit him again!"

The boy raised himself up off the ground, ran away crying, and returned with the recess duty teacher.

Pointing at George, between sobs, he said , "He hit me. He hit me," he repeated.

"Why did he hit you?" "I don't know," he lied.

The teacher faced George and asked, "Why did you hit him?"

"Butch started to fight with me. I don't know why he was fighting with me."

"Teacher, he's lying," cried Butch.

The teacher knew that the students wouldn't tell her who did what.

"O.K., you two, we are going to see Mr. Hoskins, the principal, who will get to the bottom of this melee and find out what has been going on."

"Ah, yes!" George thought to himself, "I am going to see 'Ol Halloween's' face again. I had been sent to his office so many times for 'cracking' up in class that I felt like a buddy. And now history is repeating itself--I will be in his office for the 'hundredth time."

The three entered the office. The two students sat facing the principal; the teacher, was seated on his right.

George hoped that the principal would recognize him but he was indifferent

The administrator faced the teacher, cleared his throat and in a soft fatherly voice asked, "All right Miss Windsor, what is going on?"

"These boys were fighting and when I asked who was responsible for the fight, they blamed each other. I couldn't get the truth. And you know, students never 'tattle' on other students."

In the same characteristic soft voice and half-smile, Mr. Hoskins thanked Miss Windsor and turned his attention to Butch.

"And now, young man, what is your name?"

"Joseph Josiah Larkin."

"Well, Mr. Larkin tell us what happened."

"I was playing tag with my friends and all of a sudden, he (points to George) started fighting with me."

"Then what did you do?"

"I fighted back."

"Why should this young man (points to George) start a fight with you?"

"I don't know. Maybe he hates me."

Realizing that the boy was not being truthful, the administrator turned his attention to George.

"What is your name?"

"George Lincoln Wardsworth."

He was hoping that the principal would remember him.

"Young man that is a very impressive name."

"Yes, we are the direct descendants of Abraham Lincoln."

"Now Mr. Lincoln, excuse me--Mr. Wardsworth--please tell us the truth, what really happened."

"I was walking on the playground, when Butch..."

"Who is Butch?" asked the principal.

"He is," George answered (pointing to the boy).

"When he grabbed me and started to fight, saying 'I saw you making faces at Frieda, my girl friend... I'll punch your face in."

"So what did you do?"

"I punched him."

Miss Windsor, impatiently interrupted, "Mr. Hoskins, what are we going to do?   We don't allow fighting in our school."

"Miss Windsor, I am going to tell you a story and you decide what we can do with these young people. When I was ten years old, I got into a fight with an older student . My nose was bloodied and I had a black eye, but I beat the devil out of that boy. He had a reputation of being a bully. He changed after the beating I gave him. However, I was severely punished because the boy lied and blamed me for the fight. The teacher believed the boy and she severely punished me with a wooden paddle, hitting me five time across my back. I was bed ridden for three months. I still have a reminder on my back.

"Well, Miss Windsor, what do you suggest as a punishment for these young fellows?"

"I...don't... know," she answered pensively.

"Mr. Hoskins, you decide as to what to do."

He called the two boys to the front of his desk and said, "I know, boys will be boys and I was once a boy. Shake hands and don't let it happen again.

"Oh! By the way Butch I want to talk to you. Somebody told me..."

"Excuse me, Mr. Hoskins; I am on recess duty so I better get back to the playground."

The teacher thanked the principal, left the office returning to the playground to supervise the students.

George thanked the principal, left the office, and the school. He decided to visit one more neighbor.

"For a principal, he was really is a nice fellow; it could have been worse. Guess that I misjudged him," he thought as he knocked on Mrs. Svenson's door.

The family, the parents, three sons and two daughters, had immigrated from Sweden.

A fairly heavy woman wearing a colorful apron brightly printed with a watermelon, grapes clinging on a vine, and apples; a plain skirt, and a white blouse; and a pretty brunette wearing a white blouse, Levis and an apron answered the door.

"Ya, vat is it you want, yung fello?"

"I live down the street and I wonder if you or somebody in your family remembers me."

"Oh ya, I remember yu. Yu are Armand Beliveau and yur familee leeves two blooks on Lincoln Avenue"

"No," he answered. "My name is George Lincoln Wardsworth, and I live next block on Lincoln Avenue."

A few minutes later a boy, approximately George's age, and a twin sister came to the front door and joined the family.

"What is it mama?

"Who is this boy?" asked one of the twins.

"Hilda, ths yoong feller vants to know ef yu remember him?"

"No, I don't know him."

"And you, Annette, know thees yoong feller?"

"No."

"Don't you remember, in school both of you, Katy, Maurine and I ate lunch together."

"No. Only the four of us girls eat lunch together and never ask any boy," affirmed Annette.

"Don't you remember when one of the guys took your lunch and I made him give it back to you when I told him I would beat him up if he didn't give you back your lunch?"

"No, I don't remember," answered the girl.

Disappointed, he said good bye to the Svensen family, left the house, and headed for the hospital to visit his father.

"Yes, young fellow , what can I do for you?" asked the pretty receptionist, chewing gum. "I want to see my father."

The girl reached into her mouth, retrieved the gum pasting it on the side of the reception desk and asked "What's your name?"

George was distracted by a breaking glass.

"What did you say?"

"I said: 'what is your father's name?'"

"Oh yes, his name is Joseph Washington Wardsworth."

She quickly scanned her appointment book and answered, "He is in room 103, second floor."

He climbed the stairs, entered room 103 and found two empty beds.

He returned to the reception desk. "There was nobody in the room only two empty beds." The receptionist scanned her appointment book. "Let see. Oh yes! He was transferred to room 203 this morning."

George began to doubt the girl's efficiency. He walked into room 203 and found the bed neatly made with clean fresh linen.

He walked down the hallway to another reception desk and asked, "Can you tell me what room my father, Joseph Washington Warsdworth, is in?"

The receptionist scanned her appointment book and replied, "He went into surgery this afternoon."

"How long will he be in?"

"It's hard to tell. We'll have to wait to talk to the surgeon."

George sat and waited in the hallway.

Half-an-hour later the receptionist called him and said, "Your father is in ICU. He'll be transferred to room 204 in thirty minutes."

He thanked the receptionist, waited in the hallway and half an hour later walked to room 204. Two patients, neither one his father, occupied the room.

He returned to the desk and complained that his father was not in room 204.

"There was a slight mix up but it was fixed. Your father is in room 205."

"Are you sure?"

"Yes, I am sure."

As George approached room 205, he saw in the hallway outside the room: two beds, two small tables, and chairs. Three maintenance men were working in the interior of the room. "What's wrong with the room?" George asked.

Some of the plaster fell from the ceiling and we are fixing it," answered one of the workmen, holding a paint brush.

"What happened to the patient?"

"I don't know. Hey Max, do you know what happened to the patient ?" shouted the man.

"I dono, ask the receptionist," answered the second man.

At the receptionist desk, George asked for his father's room.

The girl apologized, explaining that she just got a notice of the emergency work in room 205.

"Your father was transferred to room 207."

"These hospital people don't communicate with each other," he thought to himself.

In room 207, his father, with a full arm plaster cast, occupied one bed; a patient slept, snoring in the other. George pulled up a chair placed, it on the side close, to his father, and sat.

It was dinner time and one of the kitchen personnel delivered two trays: one she placed on a small table on his father's side; the other, on the roommate's table.

Since his father was asleep, George didn't want to waste the dinner, was hungry, and decided to eat the meal. On the tray were two covered dishes, a piece of cake, a cup of coffee, some creamer, three small paper envelopes containing salt, sugar, and pepper each separately, and a small paper cup with ketchup. He uncovered the two main dishes; one contained fried chicken; the other, three hot slices of freshly baked bread. The food was so delicious that he ate everything.

The roommate woke up and ate his dinner. "It was delicious," he commented, licking his lips with his tongue. "I didn't know that hospital food could be so tasty."

An hour later, his father began to recover from the anesthetic and saw George sitting at his side. Although he was groggy from the chemical's affect, in a forced and labored voice he asked, "Who... the... hell...are...you?"

"I am your son George."

"I don't have a son. I never had one."

"You are my father."

"Boy, don't call me father. I am not your father. Now go and find your family whoever they are. I am hungry as a bear; don't they feed the patients in this hospital?"

He picked up the phone and called the kitchen. "How about some chow. I haven't eaten a thing since I got here." The kitchen quickly delivered a tray. He "wolfed down" the food like a starved animal.

"Well, if you are not my father, and you are, I better go."

The man put his arms around George's shoulder and said," I am sorry to disappoint you, boy."

While leaving the hospital, he said good bye to his "father" and the hospital staff.

It was now 8:30 and the "ladies of the night" were parading downtown in their natural habitat, looking for their clientele to sell their wares. Some sat on bus benches, wearing miniskirts without underwear; others, leaned against street lights, wearing short shorts;. the rest of the "pack" walked up and down Main street, wearing long tight dresses to accent their figures or simple see through cotton dresses, brief bras, and bikini panties,

Drug trafficking was rampant. The police were helpless; drug dealers controlled the town. Every time the police arrested a drug dealer, he was tried, and sentenced; two drug dealers would take his place

They cruised down Main Street with impunity, looking for potential customers. Sometimes the drug dealers would knock on private doors to sell their products but the local population was not interested except for five out of the six councilmen. Former owners of the failed oil derricks, were involved in drug trafficking; the sixth member of the council owned a hardware store. Mayor Larousse was aloof to the drug problem.

The town's finances were depleted by the five councilmen's corruption: trips, vacations in expensive hotels, costly parties, and purchases of high priced condominiums.

Most of the narcotics customers were out-of-town people. Who came to enjoy themselves in the large amusement park, a source of income, located two miles from town. Four legitimate booths fronted special rooms where the illegal drugs were freely sold. It was not unusual for the police to find a dead drug dealer in an alley, lying in the gutter, shot through the head.

The girls themselves were forced to sell drugs or were motivated to sell drugs. The money they earned from drugs was theirs. They didn't have to share with anybody. High earnings enticed a large number of girls to become dealers and distributors.

One of the "ladies of the night" saw George walking down the street and she accosted him asking what was he doing down town so late at night. The boy replied that he was looking for the YMCA to spend the night.

She liked the boy and invited him to spend the night at her place where two other girls shared the apartment.

He accompanied the "lady."

On the way, she asked him, "What is your name, little man?"

George proudly said, "My name is George Lincoln Wardsworth."

"And what is your name?"

"My name is Luanna."

"That's a pretty name."

"Thank you."

They arrived at Luanna's apartment. It was rather small, one bedroom, kitchen, bath, a small side room, two couches, and a bed .in the center of the room.

The two girls were fast asleep on the couches.

When they woke up, the girls gathered around George and asked him what his name was. He proudly repeated, "George Lincoln Wardsworth."

"And what are your names?"

One of the girls answered, "I'm Delia; and" pointing to the other girl, "this is Matilda."

Luanna told George, "You see that little room, we call that the love room and you are never to go into that room. You will share a couch with Matilda and live here as long as you want to."

They loved the boy and treated him like a brother.

Periodically, each girl would bring in a client and go into the love room. George would hide in a dark corner, waiting for the girl and her client to enter the love room. The couple turned on the light and closed the door. George would walk over to the room and look through the key hole, watching the couple disrobe, and stand naked, their backs toward the door, turn out the lights, and slide into bed-- she, ready to satisfy what the man paid for.

The three girls were also heavily involved in selling narcotics. It was not unusual for them to entertain well-known dealers. One day Delia came home with a bullet wound in her shoulder. The bullet lodged just beneath her skin. Luanna, a former nurse, opened her medical bag, pulled out a pair of long tweezers, removed the bullet, and treated the wound.

"It pays to be prepared for emergencies," exclaimed Matilda.

Congratulations, Luanna, you did an excellent job," and she patted the girl's shoulder.

"OK, Delia, now tell us what happened," continued Matilda.

"Well I was buying some 'merchandise' from this creep and he quoted me a high price. I told him that it was overpriced and I wouldn't buy it. He asked me how much I thought it was worth, I quoted half the price.

The guy became angry, pulled out a gun and threatened to shoot me."

"Just for quoting a price?" asked Luanna.

"You know what these guys are like. If you don't agree with them, they threaten to kill you until you agree with them. Anyway, when the guy pulled out the gun, I jumped him and we wrestled for the gun. He accidentally pulled the trigger and it fired. I guess the barrel was pointing to his chest. He stood still for a second and I felt a sharp pain on my shoulder.

The bullet killed him, passed through his chest and became lodged in my shoulder. I placed my hand on my shoulder and saw small rivers of blood oozing out. I ripped part of my dress and applied it to my shoulder."

"You know Delia, you are lucky that you were a wrestling champion in the Olympics," assured Matilda. "Those guys are very strong.".

"You're telling me. It took all my strength to try to take the gun away," agreed Delia.

Luanna interrupted, "Delia, You need to rest and don't move that arm. We don't want you to bleed to death." .

George walked over to the girl, saying, "Let me kiss your shoulder and make you feel better."

"George, you are sweet, go ahead kiss my shoulder, and make it better."
The boy complied, Luanna administered a shot of morphine to ease the pain and Delia promptly fell asleep. Matilda busied herself at a small sewing machine making an arm sling out of some old dresses.

The "ladies of the night" are very generous. They donate thousands of dollars to schools, charitable organizations, the police and fire department. A committee was formed to make sure that all donations were properly distributed--not squandered.

Whenever an organization requests funds, the committee investigates and funds any needy or legitimate program that meets the committee's guidelines. It has to account for every dollar it spends. It has: funded schools to purchase band uniforms and instruments, sent children to summer camp, built a small family recreation park with picnic grounds and a lake for boating and swimming, constructed a heated public swimming pool, and an indoor roller and ice skating rink.

At Christmas time, the Salvation Army gets its share of the donations to feed the needy, helps the police and fire departments to distribute toys to the children of the less fortunate parents, and provides rooms for the homeless.

The next morning a radio newscaster announced: "Good morning this is station KPRQ bringing you the news.

"Mayor Larouse was killed last night between 8 and 10 P.M. by an unknown assailant. The police are investigating the crime but as yet have no clues as to who murdered the mayor or the reason for the murder.

"At 8 o'clock this morning Vice-Mayor Duffy was sworn in as the next mayor. (The voice of Mayor Duffy): "Ladies and gentlemen, as mayor of Chickasaw I promise to clean our town of the drug trade and prostitution by arresting, prosecuting, and sentencing to the full extent of the law those individuals involved.

"We can no longer see our children confronted by drug traffickers tempting them with free samples. or knocking on our doors, selling their illegal 'merchandise.' Drug peddling will be prohibited in our amusement park commonly known as 'narcotics station.'

"Narcotics make 'junkies' out of people, robbing them of their money, health, and impairing them from working or earning a living. Prostitutes break up families. Before prostitution entered our town, there was, on the average, one divorce per month. Now the divorce rate has increased tremendously. We are now known as the divorce 'capital of America.' Social and Venereal diseases have increased to epidemic proportions whereas previously it was completely eradicated. We are also faced with murders. It is not unusual to find the corpse of murdered drug dealers in our alleys.

Main Street, called, by many 'Pleasure Lane' will no longer be a hangout for prostitutes, drug dealers, and pimps. Our streets and avenues will be safe to walk. I have asked Councilmen Cally, Mathias, Hayne, and Noxon to resign or be prosecuted for drug dealing. I will clean our town and keep it clean for the sake of our children and our future generations."

"Thank you Mayor Duff and now for the weather report."

The girls turned off the radio, realizing that they faced a dim future in Chikasaw.

"Luanna, do you think Duffy means what he said?" Matilda asked bitterly.

"I have known Carl Duff since we were in kindergarten. He means what he says. Once he makes up his mind, no one can change it. So we better pack up our emergency suitcase and get ready to leave," emphasized Luanna.

Each girl had packed a suit case, which included a semi-automatic gun, and placed it near the rear entrance. Luanna packed Delia's suitcase and placed it with the other two. George was in his room and knew nothing of what was transpiring.

The following morning he was awaken by a series of gun shots and men shouting at the adjoining house.

"This is the police! Come out with your hands up!"

Several gun shots followed a staccato of gun fire then silence. The wail of an ambulance was heard as it neared the house. It had been summoned to pick up the wounded and dead.

"It's the police! Come on Matilda , let's go!" shouted Luanna.

Both girls picked up the emergency luggage, carried Delia to their van, hurriedly placed the girl in the back seat with the suit cases, went into the van and drove away.

George remained in his little room, not knowing what to do.

A series of quick door knocks echoed throughout the interior of the apartment.

"Come out with your hands up. You have one minute to come out or we shoot!" shouted the chief of police.

A minute later the police began firing. The bullets penetrated the walls targeting glass vases, mirrors big and small, ceramic plates and cups, tall and short drinking glasses, denting metal pots and pans then silence. Several bullets had penetrated George's room; one flying close to his head; another grassing his upper arm, resulting in a red mark.

The front door splintered when the police forced it open and entered the empty apartment. They began ransacking the interior. One of the policemen opened drawers and pulled out several pieces of Luanne's lingerie and showed it to another policeman.

"Look Sarge," he said, holding up a pair of bikini panties.

"Even my girlfriend wouldn't wear this and here is a bra. Boy, if it were any smaller, I doubt that it would hold anything. Whoever wore these must have been very skinny and flat cheated."

The men pulled out Delia's and Matilda's lingerie and laughingly repeated the same dialogue as they held up each piece to entertain the rest "of the boys."

A policeman knocked on George's room. He knew that if they found him, it would be off to Juvenile Hall which had a bad reputation. A small floor trap door covered the stairs to the basement. He removed the trap, climbed down the stairs, entered the cellar, stepped back up on the bottom rung of the stairs and replaced the trap door. He descended the stairs as he heard the police walking into his room, opening his chest of drawers where he kept his clothing and examining the contents, looking for narcotics. Previously George had discovered a sub cellar that was used to make liquor during prohibition. He removed a cement slab and looked around the interior of the room's sub cellar. It housed a small safe used by the girls to store narcotics.

Whenever they needed to sell some "merchandise," he was sent to the movies or some other place away from the apartment.

On the day of the police raid, he went into the basement, removed the floor slab, climbed down into the sub cellar as he gently slid back the slab in place to camouflage the entrance, turned on the light and waited.

One of the policemen descended into the basement, looked around, found some pieces of broken furniture, and climbed back out of the basement. Satisfied, the police left and the apartment was silent.

George climbed out of the sub cellar and basement and into the interior of the apartment. It looked like the "Goodwill's warehouse was hit by a windstorm." Pieces of broken furniture were everywhere. Glass, mirrors, and broken dishes covered the floor. Panties, bras, dresses, and suits had been torn into pieces and scattered. Pieces of clothing hung lazily throughout the apartment on anything that was or was not standing.

Being vigilant was utmost in his mind. He slowly looked out the .window and scouted the street making sure that the police had left the neighborhood. Once he assured himself that the 'coast was clear", he left the apartment and walked, cautiously looking around, making sure he wasn't followed.

As he turned a corner, a policeman spotted George and began following him. George ran, saw a warehouse with some empty barrels outside, and hid in one until the officer disappeared from view.

. "There must be a modern building downtown with a revolving door," he theorized.

He looked and looked and finally found a building with a revolving door. He stepped into one space and pushed the door. It turned once and stopped. George looked out of the glass enclosure and saw his and other tall office buildings he was familiar with.

He had come back to the present where he belonged. The doorman greeted him and asked, "Are you all right Mr. Wardsworth?"

George shook his hand several times and said, "Am I all right? Sure," and he hugged the doorman.

The door revolved slowly stopping three times to allow three ladies to step out of the door. He stepped out of the door, looked at the ladies and was amazed.

George exclaimed, "Clarissa, Delia, Matilda what a surprise!"

The three looked even more beautiful than when he was living with them. Their shoulder length hair was clean and neatly combed, their business suits--white or blue jacket, white long-sleeved-blouse, stockings, red white or blue suede shoes--gave them the look of a model.

He asked the second lady, "Where is Luanna?"

"Luanna who? I don't know any one named Luanna." The woman corrected him.

"I beg your pardon but my name is not Clarissa, it is Rose," explained the first lady

The second one explained that Delia was not her name, it was Jazmine.

The third advised him that her name was Hildegarde and not Matilda.

He faced Rose, went down on his knees, held her hand, and asked, "Clarissa..."

"My name is Rose," she emphasized, somewhat disturbed.

"Drusilla, Rose, whatever, will you marry me? I promised that when I was grown, I would ask you to marry me. Now I am fully grown and you also promised to marry me."

A small group of people began to gather around the couple.

"Go ahead. Say yes that you will marry each other," urged one of the onlookers.

"But I don't know you," responded Rose. "I have a boyfriend."

"Get rid of him and marry me."

Laughing, Rose said, "But it takes three days to get married, a marriage license, and a blood test."

"If we go to Las Vegas, we can be married in a day. I have a friend who is a priest, he can marry us in one day, therefore we don't have to go through all that red tape."

"I don't even know your name; I don't know who you are, and where you work."

"I have known you since I was ten years old."

She was perplexed and wondered, "How is that possible?" And asked him his name.

"George Lincoln Wardsworth," he answered. "I work in this building for Meyers, Dew, and O'Brian, in advertising."

His name sounded familiar and seemed to jog her memory as she remembered--he was the advertising genius. Everybody was talking about him and the multi-million dollar contracts with his name printed in the text she had approved. .

"Rose, what is your full name and where do you work?"

" "My name is Rose Delacrous and I work in M. D. and O.'s legal department."

"What about the other ladies?"

"They are my sisters: Jazmine is the vice-president of Babette and. Reid, Inc., international importers and exporters and Hildegarde, is the President of Electrobox. The company manufactures sensitive sophisticated electronic parts and sells exclusively to the U.S. military forces.

"Yes, I met your wonderful sisters and I was verbally spanked when I called them by the wrong name. Anyway, you and your sisters go on home and each of you pack a suitcase. We are going to go to Las Vegas to a wedding--ours! I'll meet you at the airport."

"Oh by the way, I have another sister, Anna Louise. She is a card dealer in one of the casinos. I'll ask her to meet us at the Las Vegas airport," stated Rose.

George and the girls went to their individual homes, then met at the airport, and bought tickets to Las Vegas. They boarded the jet.

After all the passengers had boarded and the freight had been loaded, the airplane began its flight.

The pilot gave the usual speech as the people sank into their assigned seats, made themselves comfortable, tightened their safety belts, and relaxed. George and Rose were occupying seats next to each other.

"You said that you have known me since you were ten years old. How is that possible?" she asked, "That's incredible."

He explained "If I told you, you wouldn't believe me. It's a long story."

The passengers' uneasiness shortened their conversations. Half-way between New York and Las Vegas, three turbaned, tanned skin individuals arose from their seats. One walked and stationed himself at the back of the aisle; and the other two at the front, each holding a gun aimed at the passengers.

One of the gunmen at the front of the aisle, suddenly turned, pushed open the cockpit door, and commandeered the plane, holding the pilot and copilot at gun point.

In broken English, one of the men shouted, "Ladies and gentlemen, stay in your seats and no one will be hurt."

George quickly realizing that it was a hijacking in process devised a plan with four male passengers: He would wrestle with and take the gun away from the hijacker stationed at the rear and create a distraction. The four passengers, two on each side aisle close to the one member of the triumvirate, would jump, disarm, and hold the criminal at gun point.

In order to carry out his plan, he needed to get close to the hijacker and did so by pretending he had to go to the facility. As soon as he was close enough to the hijacker, George shouted, "Now!" and he and the four passengers went into action disarming the hijackers and holding them at gun point.

George then forced his way into the cockpit, grabbed the hijacker by the arm and the gun fired four bullets: one wounded a male passenger in the arm; the second one, a female passenger's leg; the third, hit the pilot in the back, causing him to fall on the controls, and the fourth wounded the copilot in the arm. After a short fight George disarmed and forced the hijacker at gun point to join the other two and tied them to their seats.

He returned to the cockpit, wrapped a tourniquet on the wounded copilot's arm to stop the bleeding. Then the wounded unconscious pilot and copilot were moved out of the cockpit by several passengers. George sat in the pilot's seat, took control of the jet and with a few instructions from the tower controller, George maneuvered the plane gently down to the runway and making a perfect "three point landing." All the passengers applauded. The stewardesses were released from the facility and they advised the passengers to fasten their seat belts before landing.

An ambulance and the police were waiting for the passengers to move out before boarding the plane. On their way out the passengers shook his hand, some of the women kissed him and others handed him a business card advising him that he could visit them any time he wanted to.

The news media greeted George bombarding him with a staccato of questions:

"What is your full name?'

"George Lincoln Wardsworth."

"Was your great grandfather Abraham Lincoln?"

"Yes."

"How old are you?'

"That's not important."

"How did you do it?"

"I had no choice. I was thinking of all those people getting killed or worse."

"Do you know that you saved the lives of 129 passengers?"

"Yes, something like that."

"Weren't you afraid of getting killed?"

"When you are in such a situation, you only think about surviving."

"How did you feel when you were taking the gun away from the hijacker?"

"Afraid."

"You know everybody all over America thinks of you as a hero. How do you feel about being a hero?"

"I feel flattered."

Rose greeted her sister, Anna Louise, and the four beautiful girls stood next to George, Rose holding his hand.

One of the reporters asked Rose, "What do you plan to do in Las Vegas?"

She replied, "I am going to marry my Hero!"

###

ABOUT THE AUTHORS:
Riette Suzzette Ormond
and
George Ormond

Riette Suzzette, French, a former fashion model, vocalist, ballroom dancer, and stand-up comedienne enjoys performing as a 6-year-old little girl: "SWEET BABY SUZZETTE," who views the world in all its innocence from a family orientated situation.

She attended the University of Southern California, and subsequently graduated from San Diego State University with a B.A. degree in journalism and minors in public relations and photography.

Mrs. Ormond is a professional photographer and artist, specializing in oils and watercolors. She is being urged to have a one-woman show of her paintings and photographs.

George Ormond was born in Paris, France, resided in Vera Cruz, Mexico, educated in the United States, and graduated with 3 degrees and 6 majors from the University of Southern California. He is a life-time alumni member of both U.S.C. and Alpha Kappa PSI, honorary business fraternity.

They met at a University of Southern California, Los Angeles, California, dance and were married shortly thereafter.

George is a great perfumer. He has perfected 19 pure, fabulous perfumes including Chocolate Valentine, Vanilla Moonlight, Rose, Gardenia, Lilac, Mango, Mimosa, etc.

He has also perfected a Wonder Cream that is great as a skin moisturizer and promotes the growth of stronger, longer finger nails. One day, his wife said, "I have natural curly hair" and he perfected a hair conditioner.

George began entertaining when five years old in Vera Cruz, dancing the Jarabe Tapatio (the popular Mexican Hat Dance) around an oversized sombrero.

Riette Suzzette's first performing experience took place when she was requested to sing in front of a live audience at the age of five.

The Ormond's have always enjoyed doing stand-up comedy and exhibition ballroom dancing; George writes the singular and duo comedy acts and choreographs their dance routines

It was a happy day and a complete surprise when CUDDLES, their lovable baby goose, turned out to be a "ham," sparkling in front of the camera, a live audience, and charming everyone with her ability to laugh and answer questions.

When they realized that CUDDLES was a very special goose and enjoyed performing, she became a very important part of their act, delivering singing telegrams.

Cuddles loves to dress-up and looks adorable wearing her red and white polka dot dress, red panties with white lace ruffles, matching booties, and bonnet.

They were asked to be in the pilot of the "New Gong Show" and the "El Gong Show" with Cuddles. They had won several years earlier dancing on the "Gong Show," and the producer had called and requested that they return for numerous engagements on the show. They've performed and been interviewed on television, radio, movies, parades, and in print.

It is always a pleasure to perform with Cuddles, delivering a singing telegram on birthdays, anniversaries, graduations, Christmas, and other parties for children, adults, U.S.O., parades, etc.

And, NOW, there is a new family member that they rescued, a cocker spaniel poodle that Riette Suzzette's darling husband, George, named Yammy Yogurt.

NOTES